Tom has always made his living from words, firstly in publishing, and later in advertising and public relations. His debut novel, *Lost & Found,* was published in five languages. He lives in Berlin, with a potted plant and a variety of noisy neighbours.

Also by Tom Winter

Lost & Found

Arms Wide Open

TOM WINTER

31 DAYS OF WONDER

corsair

CORSAIR

First published in Great Britain in 2017 by Corsair

1 3 5 7 9 10 8 6 4 2

Copyright © Tom Winter, 2017

The moral right of the author has been asserted.

A CIP catalogue record for this book
is available from the British Library.

ISBN: 978-1-4721-5316-6

Typeset in Bembo by SX Composing DTP, Rayleigh, Essex
Printed and bound in Great Britain by Clays Ltd, St Ives plc

Papers used by Corsair are from well-managed forests
and other responsible sources.

MIX
Paper from
responsible sources
FSC
www.fsc.org   FSC® C104740

For A. F. Rodda
With all my thanks

Grosvenor Square Garden, London W1

It began like all Ben's conversations. Badly.

Until he saw her, it was just another day in Grosvenor Square. It was people, and sunshine, and grass just the right shade of green. It was the first daffodils of spring, and birdsong in the heart of Mayfair. And then he spied her: a young woman sitting alone on a bench, her yellow dress appearing to glow in the lunchtime sun; her fuller figure suggestive of a fuller life, a bigger heart.

Perhaps if Ben was more discreet – had any capacity for discretion, in fact – he might have just lingered there, surreptitiously admiring her from behind the statue of Roosevelt or one of the park's bulbous plane trees, but no – as soon as he sees her, his feet are carrying him closer and closer, sweeping him across the park on a wave of joy he's never felt before, his mouth filling with words so quickly that his mind has no time to review them first. It's only as he's standing there right in front of her that consciousness begins to catch up with him. Although he can't be sure what he's just said, he gets the uneasy feeling that it included something about his grandmother being prone to hot flushes.

'Whatever I just said, ignore it. Unless it was, you know, *normal*, in which case don't.' He takes a deep breath, worried that he's failing to make a good first impression. 'What I'm trying to say is, I'm Ben. And I think you're beautiful. Very, very beautiful.'

She smiles now – a smile that makes the world feel like a better, warmer place – and Ben starts to forget himself all over again, the words flowing like water.

It's an older woman who brings his reverie to an end. 'Alice,' says the intruder, cutting between them, 'what's going on here?'

'Don't worry,' says Ben, 'we're just chatting.' Or at least that's what he thinks he said; his heart is racing so fast, it's impossible to know for sure. 'Me and my motor mouth,' he says, with a laugh. 'Imagine how bad I'd be if I *wasn't* on medication.'

The older woman looks aghast. 'We should be getting you back to Glasgow,' she says, urging Alice from the bench.

'You live in Glasgow?' says Ben.

Alice is about to say something, but the older woman cuts in. 'Yes, she does. And it's time she got back there.'

Getting up now, Alice gives him an apologetic smile. 'It was very nice to meet you,' she says, as she's herded away.

They're some distance off, Ben still watching them go, when Alice glances back and smiles again. And in that instant, he knows in his heart that today is a momentous day; come what may, he and Alice will meet again, and life will never be the same.

20 minutes later

Alone in the office toilets, Alice stands in front of the mirror, tries to see in herself what Ben saw; to understand how his face could light up at the sight of her, when all she can see is fat. Turning first this way and then that, she searches for a flattering angle; is facing away from the mirror, peering back over her shoulder, squinting through one eye, when one of her many well-heeled colleagues, Lucy, enters the room. She joins Alice in front of the mirror, touches up her perfect lipstick.

'Do you think I've gained weight?' Alice asks her.

'Oh, Alice,' Lucy replies, genuine warmth in her voice, 'of course you have, but you don't need to worry about that.'

'Said the size two.'

'But you're not like the rest of us, you know that. I was talking to a friend about this the other day; how I've discovered an entirely different view of life since you started working here.' She becomes more animated. 'It's a bit like that moment in *The Hunchback of Notre Dame* where you realize that Quasimodo isn't just some evil, deformed dwarf, but has human qualities too. It's really touching.'

With a sweet smile – doubtless feeling, in fact, that she's just been *supportive* – Lucy heads for the door. Not wanting to look at her reflection again, Alice too leaves the room, trying to walk with Lucy's self-assurance; trying to imagine the time when she will also be strutting around in expensive clothes, her days as a bullied and badly paid intern a long distant memory.

*

Alice returns to her desk to find her boss, Geneva, staring across the office.

'Is everything all right?' says Alice.

'Glasgow's up to something.'

'I think we should stop calling him that.'

Geneva ignores her. 'Look at him. Strutting around like the proverbial peacock.'

Alice follows her gaze, watches as the managing director, Piers, talks to one of their colleagues on the far side of the room.

'I've always thought he's rather handsome,' says Alice.

'I can see how someone like *you* would be impressed. He knows how to charm, I'll give him that. But I can assure you, if you look past the rakish hair and expensive tailoring, he's Glasgow through and through.'

'He's not even Scottish.'

'But go back forty years and all you'll find is a tenement slum.' Geneva looks away now, as though the very sight of him has become distasteful. 'Let's put it this way, I doubt any of his grandparents ever held a pen.'

'Even if that's true, shouldn't we be encouraging social mobility?'

Geneva snorts. 'Is that what you were doing with that strange man in the park today?'

'He wasn't strange.'

'Alice, I had to rescue you.'

'No, you didn't. He was sweet. He was saying some really lovely—'

She's interrupted by the sound of canine retching. On the floor between them, Geneva's dog, a stick-thin Italian greyhound, is in the middle of yet another purge.

'Oh, poor Harry,' says Geneva, backing away from him. 'It was probably that kale smoothie he had for lunch.'

Alice stares at the mess of thick green liquid pooling on the floor. 'I'm not sure that's the kind of thing you can give to a dog.'

'I thought it might help him detox. Though I suppose in some ways it did.' She gives Alice the first smile of the day. 'You know I'm totally useless at these things. Would you be a darling?'

Brixton, London SW2
4 miles from Alice

Ben drifts home in a daze, only vaguely aware that he may have forgotten something important.

'I'm going to Scotland,' he shouts, as he opens the front door. 'Dave? Did you hear me? I'm going to Glasgow.'

His flatmate calls back to him from the living room. 'Why aren't you at work?'

Ben follows the sound of Dave's voice, finds him making candles at the dining table, his paraphernalia looking so much like a meth factory, he keeps the curtains closed even in the daytime.

Ben speaks again. 'I'm going to—'

'I thought you were working all day.'

'That's it! I knew I'd forgotten something.'

'Ben...'

'I met a beautiful woman in the park.'

'That's okay, then. Your boss is sure to understand.'

'Do you think so?'

'No! You're already lucky they haven't fired you.'

'What does it matter? I'll have to quit the job anyway. I'm off to Glasgow.'

'Have you stopped taking your medication?'

'There's nothing wrong with my meds, thank you very much. Her name's Alice. She's beautiful, and special, and leaving for Glasgow is the right thing to do.'

'Ben, do you remember that time you painted your bedroom orange because you thought it was the right thing to do?' Ben wanders into the kitchen in search of food, Dave shouting to him through the wall. 'And then, when you decided you didn't like it after all, do you recall how many coats of paint it took to get it white again?'

'This is different,' shouts Ben, rummaging through the fridge.

'Or how about that time you got a buzz cut because you thought it would look good?'

He wanders back to Dave, eating straight from a tub of cream cheese. 'Jake Gyllenhaal looked great in *Southpaw*.'

'Mate, I could hear you crying in your room. For two days.'

Ben speaks through a full mouth. 'So do you fancy coming to Scotland with me?'

'Her name's Alice, right? Alice what?'

7

Ben hesitates. 'Does that matter?'

'Be honest, did you actually talk to her or just learn her name from loitering?'

'We spoke, thank you. And it was this other woman who told me she lives in Glasgow. Some uptight bird with an anorexic dog.'

'So Ben, ask yourself: why was Alice sitting in a park in London if she lives in Glasgow?'

'All these questions! It's no wonder you're still single.' He scrapes out the last of the cream cheese, sucks it from his spoon. 'And your candles smell like mouthwash, by the way.'

'They're clove and mint. I think they'll sell well at the market on Saturday.'

'I doubt that very much.'

Dave lets the comment go, appears accustomed to them. 'Look, I just want you to think about the conversations we've had in the past. About making rash decisions. It sounds like you barely talked to her.'

'I didn't need to. I knew it, I *felt* it. She smiled at me.'

'Ben, this is England. A smile can mean "Piss off, I hate you".'

'Don't worry,' says Ben, raising his voice as he leaves the room again. 'I know you're only trying to protect—' He comes face to face with Alice, cooking in the kitchen; screams at the sight of her.

'Are you all right in there?' calls Dave. Alice raises a finger to her lips, she and Ben sharing a secret moment. 'Ben?' calls Dave again.

'It's nothing,' he croaks. 'Everything's fine.' He watches as Alice spoons cookie dough onto a baking sheet, appearing to take endless pleasure in the task. Still smiling, she offers Ben a spoonful of dough. Nervous, hopeful, he reaches for it, but then pulls his hand back. 'Oh, God,' he says, to himself. 'This can't be a good sign.'

'Mate, what did you say?'

Ben slowly backs from the room. Heart pounding, eyes wide, he returns to Dave, sits down at the table.

'Are you sure you're okay?' says Dave.

'Yeah,' replies Ben. 'I'm, er, I'm just thinking about that girl, aren't I?'

'And that's my point, mate. I know you're intent on seeing her—'

'Seeing her? Who said anything about seeing her?'

'*You* did, Ben. You said you're going up to Glasgow.' He starts pouring molten wax into candle moulds. 'I just don't want you making any rash decisions, that's all. There's your job to think about, not to mention all the cost and aggravation of a wasted trip. And you know how you are sometimes, tuning out important details.' Ben's attention drifts towards the kitchen, barely hearing what Dave's saying. '… promise me… at least a few days… talk it over… Ben?' Louder now. 'Ben?' Dave is staring at him, appears concerned. 'Mate, are you sure you're all right?'

Ben struggles to keep his eyes on Dave. 'I'm fine,' he says, labouring over the words, wishing them to be true. 'There's absolutely nothing to worry about at all.'

Camberwell, London SE5

3½ miles from Alice

It's the usual weekday morning in the doctor's waiting room: people of all ages gently coughing and sneezing into dog-eared copies of *Woman's Own* and *House & Garden*. On the few occasions that Ben's come here – always to replace a lost prescription – he and Dr Glover have struck up an easy-going familiarity. Perhaps relieved that Ben doesn't come with a communicable disease, the doctor's always taken a little longer over the consultation, happy to spend a few extra minutes discussing the weather or some such. Today, when Ben's turn comes, he finds Dr Glover looking much older than on his last visit. Unlike the room, its functional furniture and cautionary posters appearing untouched by time, Dr Glover seems to have been ravaged by the passing months: his thick auburn hair has already gone, replaced by a monochromatic tide reaching outwards from his scalp, as though his head is filled with grey, and life is now squeezing it from him like toothpaste.

'Benjamin,' he says, already reaching for his pad. 'Have you lost your prescription again?'

'Actually,' he replies, 'I wanted to have a chat.' He glances up, heartened to see that a few of the ceiling tiles still point in the wrong direction; odd ones out, just like him. He looks back at Dr Glover, ready to say what's on his mind – *I'm seeing*

13

things, I'm going mad – but finds himself distracted. 'You're looking so old. It's like you're ageing in cat years.'

For an instant, Dr Glover appears speechless, and Ben worries that his well-intentioned honesty has once again blown a hole in the fabric of everyday life. 'It's divorce,' Dr Glover says, finally. 'A bloody mess, the lot of it. When you love someone, but they say they don't love you anymore...' He sighs, looking so down it's easy to imagine that *he's* the patient, sitting there with Ben in the hope of getting a pill that will take away all the pain. 'But we shouldn't be talking about that,' he says, seeming to rally. 'What is it you wanted to discuss?'

'I, er, wanted to talk about love, but maybe this is the wrong time.'

'Not at all, Benjamin. Just because my own marriage has descended into... bitter recriminations and outright lies.' Another sigh. 'Have you met someone?'

'Yeah, but I'm worried that I'm becoming a bit, I don't know, obsessed.'

'Is that what she's told you?' He doesn't even wait for an answer. 'Because it happens, I know that from my own experience. What a man might think is sweet and romantic, a woman just dismisses as creepy and inappropriate.'

Ben is distracted by the gentle opening of the office door, and Alice tiptoeing into the room. Panicked, he tries to focus on Dr Glover; on the flashing of his white teeth as words of wisdom spill forth. '... love is a powerful drug... disorienting... despite what my wife says... perfectly normal...' Standing behind Dr Glover now, Alice takes a bag of lemon bonbons from her pocket, offers one to Ben. Looking away, he tries even harder to focus on Dr Glover, his brow becoming furrowed with the effort. 'Benjamin, is everything all right? You seem a little overwhelmed.'

'Can I be completely honest?'

14

'You can say anything in here.'

'I just feel like she's with me. Like she's right here in the room.'

'That's excellent!'

'Really?' He glances at Alice again, a broad smile on her face. 'Then why does it feel like madness?'

'Because love *is* madness, but the very best kind!'

'This isn't at all what I thought you'd say. I thought it was a problem with my medication.'

'Have you experienced anything else that would suggest that? Any depressive or manic episodes? Any physical symptoms?'

Ben shakes his head. 'Everything's been good.'

'Then there's nothing to worry about!' Dr Glover leans forward in his seat, his tone becoming more passionate. 'You've got to be open to love, Ben. That's what I've been trying to tell my wife for the last six months. Yes, love can be messy and frightening, but you can't just give up and run away. You have to embrace it. And if you think you're losing your mind in the process, well, maybe that's a good thing. Does this young woman like you as much as you like her?'

Alice still stands there, beaming at Ben. 'Yeah, I would say so.'

'Then go for it! When love is staring you in the face, you'd be mad not to.'

'I think we can safely say that it really is staring me in the face.'

'Then I'm thrilled for you, I honestly am. And I say that both as your doctor and as your friend.' He nods to himself, clearly pleased with his own counsel. 'It's only when we can *see* the love that's right in front of us that we can truly find happiness.'

Soho, London W1

'You don't have to eat a salad,' says Alice's best friend, Rachel.

'Trust me,' replies Alice, 'if this was a nudist beach, you'd

15

realize I do.' She eats a forkful of cold, damp leaves; tries not to look as Rachel takes her first bite of pizza. 'When I'm the all-new svelte version of me, I'll be glad I made this sacrifice.'

'Have your colleagues been making comments again?'

'When don't they? I swear they're all so perfect, it's like they're from the same factory.' She searches her plate for something, anything, other than lettuce. 'I'm so clearly the odd one out, I sometimes get the feeling they only offered me the job as a sort of private sport, like twenty-first-century bear baiting.'

'You're nowhere near as fat as a bear.'

'That wasn't actually my point, but thank you; after a week like mine, I'll take compliments wherever I can find them.' She stabs at more lettuce leaves. 'How are the job applications?'

'I'm still hopeful that I'll get a recording contract any day now.' Alice chooses this moment to take a diplomatic sip of her lemonade. *I would agree with you, but see, I can't, I'm drinking.* 'Imagine, I could become a pop star without ever having experienced the dreaded day job. I'll be able to move out of my parents' place and into a mansion.' Rachel appears to be waiting for a response, but Alice keeps sucking on her straw. 'If you quit your job too, we can follow our dreams together.'

'I am following my dream,' replies Alice. 'I could do without cleaning up dog puke, but let's face it, that's probably the best possible training for a career in PR.' She stares at Rachel's pizza, so distracted by it she forgets what she was saying. Rachel takes a slice, puts it on Alice's salad. 'No, I shouldn't,' says Alice.

'I just want you to be happy.' She passes her yet another slice, instantly transforming a sparse salad into a towering heap of salami and melted cheese. 'Personally, I think you're the ideal weight.'

'Ideal for a wrestler, perhaps, but my ambition in life goes beyond wanting to choke someone to death with bingo wings.' And now Rachel hands her a third slice too. 'No, that's too much. There'll be nothing left for you.'

'It's all right. It's a good excuse to try something I've been practising at home.' She waves to a nearby waiter. 'Watch this,' she says to Alice. As the waiter reaches their table, she breaks into high-pitched vocals, singing her request in a very bad impression of Whitney Houston. 'I'llllll taaaaake sommmmmme gaaaarrrrrlic breeeeeaaaaad, pleeeeaaase.' He stares at her, appears to have been rendered speechless by the horror of it. 'Did you see his expression?' says Rachel, as he finally walks away. 'Now imagine that on the faces of thirty thousand people.'

'That would really be… something,' says Alice, reaching for her drink again.

'I'd like us to make another video this weekend. I think this might be the one that goes viral.' Alice sucks on her straw, but gets only the rattle of an empty glass. 'When are you free?'

'Well, you know I'm—'

'You've already said you're not working this weekend.'

'Yeah, but I'll be at my parents' place on Sunday.'

'That's fine, we can do it tomorrow. I was thinking we could record it in the toilet this time. The acoustics in there are—'

'I can't,' says Alice, the words rushing out before she's even considered the consequences. 'I have a date.'

Stunned silence.

'What's his name?' says Rachel.

'Er, Ben.'

Rachel leans back in her seat, has clearly decided that Ben is an interloper. 'And how come you've never mentioned him before?'

'We only met yesterday. In the park, believe it or not.' She smiles, not at the memory, but with relief at being able to say something truthful. 'We chatted briefly and, well, you know…'

17

'Really, Alice, it sometimes feels like you never tell me anything.'

'It was only yesterday.'

'I suppose I can find a way to make the video myself.' She starts picking at her food. 'But I want to hear all about your date,' she adds, her tone now sounding more interrogative than gossipy. 'I want to hear every last detail.'

Lewisham Market, London SE13

17 miles from Alice

It's a slow morning at the market, most people looking a little too hungover to buy anything other than bacon sandwiches and cups of coffee. Ben stares at the people milling past, both hopeful and yet terrified that Alice will appear at any second.

'Are you okay?' says Dave.

'Yes,' replies Ben, a little too quickly. 'Why wouldn't I be?'

'It's just you've seemed a bit distracted for the last couple of days. Almost like you're looking for something.'

'I'm distracted by Alice, aren't I?' He tries to focus on Dave, but still his gaze keeps drifting to the passers-by, no one taking an interest in their stall. 'Just because I can, you know, *see* the love in front of me, there's nothing wrong with that. It's the best kind of madness.'

'Well, things are sure to pick up around here once everyone's had some breakfast. That'll help to take your mind off it.'

'I doubt it, mate. No one wants candles like these.'

'They aren't for everyone, Ben, they're for connoisseurs.'

'Have you decided if you're coming to Scotland with me?'

'I thought we'd established that you know nothing about this woman?'

'I know her name's Alice. How many can there be in Glasgow? Anyway, if you'd seen her, you'd know that I've got to find her again. She's like a TV commercial for fabric softener. All soft woolly jumpers, and puppies running through flower meadows. She likes to bake cookies, too.'

'How do you know that?'

'She, er, mentioned it, didn't she?'

'In the space of your ten-second conversation?'

A young woman stops to sniff one of the candles.

'It's bloody awful, isn't it?' says Ben, relieved at the distraction. 'Take it from me, if you burn one of those at home, you'll get a nose bleed, you'll go blind.' The woman puts it down and moves on. 'She obviously wasn't a *connoisseur*.'

'Ben, I never asked you to be here.'

'You don't like being here on your own.'

'I'm not going to be on my own. Agnes is coming. It's just punctuality's not her thing, you know that.' He digs in one of his pockets, offers Ben some cash. 'Here, go and get yourself a cup of coffee.'

'I can't take your money. You haven't sold anything.'

'It's okay, I had a good week last week.'

'Then why didn't you just make the same candles? That's stupid.' Dave is staring at him now, and Ben gets the feeling that he may have said too much. 'You know what? A coffee's not a bad idea. Thanks.'

*

Aware that Dave probably doesn't want him back anytime soon, Ben drifts with the crowd. As so often happens at the market, his perambulations end at the stall of Indian spices, its many pots of multi-coloured powders enveloping him in their fragrance, the middle-aged owner drifting around in a bright red sari.

'Hello,' she says. 'It's nice to see you again.'

Standing there, Ben wishes that he could say the things he wants to say, rather than only saying things he wishes he hadn't. *When I was young, my parents died in India*, he would tell her. *It would be nice if you could make me a curry. I could close my eyes while I eat it and imagine that I'm there with them.*

Panicked, he turns his attention to the spices instead. 'I'm seeing my gran this afternoon. I was, er, thinking of getting her something.'

'Does she like to cook?'

'Well, she cooks, after a fashion. Though I'm not sure she *likes* it.'

'But she likes Indian food?'

'Probably not,' Ben mumbles, already backing away. 'Maybe this wasn't such a good idea.'

'How about some Himalayan salt?' she says, holding up a small bag of pink crystals. 'Everyone loves salt.'

'Yeah, but she's got high blood pressure or something. I think salt might kill her.' He stands at a distance, as though the salt might kill him too. 'It's nothing personal,' he says, wishing they could start all over again. 'Maybe I'll come back another week.'

And still she smiles, her face creasing into soft folds. 'You have a stall on the other side of the market, don't you? The candles look nice.'

'My mate, Dave, makes them. They're a bit crap, to be honest, but he's a good bloke.'

'Here,' she says, holding out the salt. 'It's a gift. From one stallholder to another.'

Ben finally comes forward. 'Thank you,' he says, so self-conscious that, as soon as he's taken it, he turns on his heels and scurries back into the crowd.

24 miles from Alice and counting

Ben gazes out at the passing scenery, the bag of salt still in his hands. It's always the early years that he thinks of when he travels out to his grandparents' house: trying to recall how this

23

journey felt to him as a five-year-old child, doubtless marvelling at the overnight transformation from India's sun-baked earth to this damp green landscape; hopeful, as only a young child can be, that the same transformation may yet be worked on his parents, their bodies still lying in an Indian morgue. And then the hushed new existence that unfolded over the following years: sharing a silent house with two elderly people he'd never met before, unable to see anything of himself in their wrinkled faces and quiet self-discipline.

Alice's voice rouses him from his thoughts. 'It's a lovely view, isn't it?' He looks up to find her sitting in the opposite seat, her yellow dress seeming to shine like the sun.

'You're not real,' he says, in a loud whisper. He glances around the carriage, no one in earshot. 'I don't care what Dr Glover says. I know you're just in my head.'

'That's surely real enough?' she replies, smiling.

'Is this going to stop if I come and find you in Glasgow? Or am I just going to end up with two of you?'

'There's only one of me, Ben, I promise you that.' She takes a small paper bag from her pocket. 'Would you like a lemon bonbon? Everyone likes a bonbon.' She pops one in her mouth, her smile growing even wider. 'Yellow is my favourite colour.'

'You do seem to wear a lot of it.'

'It's just such a happy colour, don't you think?' She leans down to take a closer look at his bag of salt. 'Though, I must say, that's a very pretty shade of pink.'

From the far end of the carriage, another voice. 'Tickets, please.'

Ben turns to watch as the ticket inspector makes her way up the aisle; he speaks to Alice without looking at her. 'She won't be able to see you, will she?'

'Please don't be sad about the past.'

'How do you know about that?' he says, turning to face her, but she's already gone.

24

Ben looks for Alice when he gets off at Maidstone, spending a little too long glancing up and down the platform, wondering if he might spot her among the many other passengers getting off there. The train is already pulling away when he realizes that he's the last one on the platform, his grandfather watching him from the exit. Ben's told him countless times that he can make his own way to the house, but still his grandfather insists on coming to meet him, always standing right there by the platform, as if he doesn't even trust Ben to find his way to the car park alone.

On this occasion he looks vaguely alarmed by Ben's behaviour. 'Don't worry, Granddad, nothing's wrong. I, er, I bumped into a friend on the train. I thought she was getting off here too.' He glances again at the empty platform. 'I guess not.'

With a mere nod, his grandfather heads for the car, Ben walking a few steps behind. When Ben was still a child, he learnt that his grandfather had been drafted into the Korean War and 'seen some terrible things'. Even now, all these years later, it seems like his grandfather's mind is forever back in 1950s Korea, so that even the sleepy streets of the Kent commuter belt hide the constant threat of landmines and snipers; every journey made in an understandably tense silence.

His grandfather only speaks as they pull up in front of their bungalow, Ben's gran already coming out to meet them, looking even smaller and thinner than on his last visit.

'She's getting more frail,' his grandfather says, the words so soft, it's hard to know if he's speaking to Ben or simply thinking aloud. 'But she's still with us. For now, at least.'

'Benjamin, how are you?' she says, calling to him through the window. As he opens the car door, there's a loud squawk from the house. 'And Neville's missed you,' she says, excitedly. 'He'll be so pleased.'

She leads Ben inside, the squawks growing louder with every step. Upon entering the living room, Neville, an African grey parrot, explodes into a shrill torrent, rocking violently against the bars, one bulging eye trained on Ben.

'Would you listen to that?' says Ben's grandmother, beaming. 'He's been so quiet all morning. He must be happy to see you.'

Looking at Neville, this seems doubtful. The sound he's making is much how Ben imagines a difficult exorcism: the possessed child kept locked in a cage while he spits and screams about Satan.

Yet still his grandmother looks delighted. 'It's nice to have something lively in the house, don't you think?'

'You never said that when I was young.'

'Oh, you were already a man when you arrived.'

'I was five.'

'Yes, but Neville here, he's…' Her face lights up with a joy that Ben can only describe as maternal. 'He's a *baby*.'

*

Exhausted by hatred, Neville sleeps while Ben and his grandparents eat. Although his grandmother has never been a skilled cook, her repertoire has grown ever more limited as she's aged. Today, they sit down to a meal of cheese on toast, the edges of the bread burnt and blackened.

Ben's grandfather sits in silence, the look on his face suggesting that his mind is still elsewhere: wading through rice paddies, perhaps; a convenient distraction from the food.

'I met a beautiful girl the other day,' says Ben, choosing not to mention that he's been hallucinating her ever since.

'How lovely,' replies his grandmother. 'In my day, if a man wasn't married with kids by the time he was your age…'

'Gran, I'm only twenty-three.'

'Still, we would have just come to other conclusions.' She pats his hand. 'And I want to say, Benjamin, it really doesn't matter. I mean, you know…' She lowers her voice. 'If you prefer willy.'

Ben notices his grandfather stiffen. 'No, Gran, it's nothing like that.'

'There's no need to feel ashamed, Benjamin. The world's changed.'

'I'm planning to go and see her, up in Glasgow.'

'Well…' Her smile becomes vacant. 'Were you saying something?'

'That I'm going to Glasgow.'

'Why on earth would you want to do that?'

'For the girl I've met. She lives there.'

'My, my,' she replies, clearly unable to remember anything about the conversation. 'Glasgow's a long way, but I suppose absence makes the heart grow fonder.'

Neville chooses this moment to wake up and prove her wrong, emitting a squawk that's so shrill, so panicked, Ben drops what he's eating, and even his grandfather looks startled. For a few seconds, he stares at his plate, as though Neville's cries have reminded him of some terrible wartime atrocity.

'I forgot to buy him bananas,' he says, finally. 'He likes bananas.'

*

As always on these visits, Ben dedicates some time to flicking through the family photo album. Even though he knows its contents by heart, he still turns the pages with bated breath, as if today might be the day that he finds some long lost picture of his parents. In many ways, the album reveals more by the things it doesn't contain than the things it does: the first five or six pages are full of his grandparents in the early days of their marriage, his grandfather the same stiff man that he is today, albeit encased in smooth skin and with a fine head of hair. The final picture from those youthful years is Ben's grandmother, heavily pregnant, their whole world on the cusp of change.

And then, nothing. A tell-tale absence.

That's the thing about hate, thinks Ben, as he flicks through the empty pages that follow: it doesn't leave a photographic record. His father despised his parents so much, he destroyed every photo of himself before leaving home, and they never saw fit to refill those blank pages, perhaps feeling that the emptiness was the only thing they had left of him. Having removed all traces of his existence, Ben's father walked away never to see them again, no thought that years later his own son would return in his place, a mere five-year-old boy, his entire history erased.

When Ben had first arrived, there was hope that his mother's family would offer some support and kinship, but then it became apparent that she too had been orphaned at an early age, no family left to find. In the years since, it's often seemed to Ben that that was her only legacy: an inheritance of misfortune; this woman whom he wouldn't even recognize if he saw her in a picture.

After years of blank pages, that's where the photo album bursts back into life: Ben newly embedded with his grandparents, everyone looking a little dazed. There are only a few pictures of Ben as a child, neither of his grandparents realizing at the time that his young mind was already misfiring and knitting itself into strange new patterns; yet another loss for two ageing people who'd already lost so much. After the age of ten or eleven, there are no more photos, their disappointment perhaps too painful to record. The rest of the album sits empty, all attempts at family life fading into black.

By contrast, his grandmother's mail-order catalogue offers comfort in abundance: page after colourful page of smiling people living perfect lives. Years of his childhood were spent poring over pages just like these, imagining that the people in the pictures were his real family – smiling at one another as they barbecued steaks in front of their brand-new tent;

running together into the sea while wearing this season's latest swimwear.

He's not even aware of his grandmother's presence until she speaks. 'If you see anything you like, I can order it for you.'

'I like too much,' he replies, 'that's the problem.' He touches the pages as he says it, not wanting the lawnmowers and inflatable paddling pools, but rather to be one of those people: to be someone who never says or does the wrong thing; to be the kind of person who looks into a camera and laughs, as if every moment in life is easy.

His grandmother speaks again. 'I'm going to make some coffee, if you want some. It's instantaneous powder. Really amazing stuff. You just add water and hey presto, it's done.'

'No, thanks, Gran, I should be getting home soon.' And as he says it, he thinks of Alice: that even though she's out there somewhere, under the same sky as him, everything else about her – how she lives and what she did today – all remain a mystery.

Feltham, West London

Opportunities to be more assertive...

Alice considers the words, decides that they lack assertive-ness.

MY ACTION PLAN! How I'm going to transform my life...

1. **Politely tell Mei that 7:30 on a Sunday morning is too early to be cleaning the flat.**

She listens to the castrated wailing of the vacuum cleaner as Mei, her flatmate, drags it from room to room.

2. **Consider skipping breakfast from now on. Or lunch. Maybe even both. Hungry people are slimmer people!**

As the noise grows louder and her stomach begins to growl, Alice pulls the bedcovers over her head, tries to imagine what it would be like to have her own apartment; a place in which she could greet each day in pure silence, perhaps spending the first hour of every morning in a variety of yoga poses, while sipping wheatgrass juice.

And now the vacuum cleaner is ramming against her bed-room door – once, twice, three times – the scream of the motor rising and falling as it's jerked back and forth.

Unable to think, let alone sleep, she goes out to the hallway just in time to see Mei introducing the vacuum cleaner to the bathroom door, the whole thing rattling on its hinges.

'Mei,' she says, raising her voice over the din. 'Mei.'

Mei glances at her. 'I thought you were sleeping,' she shouts.

Alice forces a smile, tries to remember how Mei was when they first met almost one year ago: a shy young student who'd just arrived from Shanghai, her English vocabulary limited almost entirely to *yes*, *please* and *thank you*, with nothing but blushes and self-conscious giggles to fill the gaps. In retrospect, Alice can see that she mistook language skills for personality, like listening to Hitler speak in fumbling English and assuming him to be a sweet man. She can barely admit it to herself now, but back then Mei didn't just seem to be the perfect flatmate, she was going to be a *project*. In the same way that people get a puppy and imagine all the long walks they'll take together, Alice would often picture herself introducing Mei to the very best of England: a well-rounded education of museums, country pubs and fine ale.

She can see now that she was right to think of Mei as a puppy. After nearly a year of living together, Mei has long since grown into something less easy to love – a dangerous mastiff, a rabid pit bull – so that Alice often fantasizes about driving her to some distant town and leaving her on the roadside, or even taking her to the vet and simply having her put down.

From upstairs, a violin bursts into life; not the mournful beauty of Bach, but rather the repetitive *do-re-mi* of someone scratching out their contempt for the world and everything in it.

Mei glances at the ceiling, shouts over the roar of the vacuum cleaner. 'One day, I'm going up there with a broken bottle. I'm going to fuck him up.'

The 10:44 to Wickford, Essex

Although she's spent almost an hour crossing London, it's only as Alice's train is pulling out of Liverpool Street that she starts

34

to panic; tries to reassure herself that she'll have a lovely day at her parents' house, even though she's told herself this on many previous occasions and it's never once been true. She stares out of the window, watching as London's gritty East End begins to morph into something more sedate and suburban; the carapace of her urban life slowly being torn away.

Rachel inevitably provides some distraction; the train is pushing into open countryside when she sends her first message of the day: *'How did it go with Ben? Tell ALL.'*

'Nothing to tell,' Alice writes back, hopeful that she'll be allowed to leave it there, at a statement of truth.

Seconds later, her phone rings. 'There can't be nothing to tell,' says Rachel, as soon as Alice answers. 'You went on a date. By definition, that means there's something to tell.'

'Is the thought of me going on a date really that remarkable?'

'Yes. Where are you? Let's meet.'

'I'm on the way to my parents' place.'

'Then at least tell me something about yesterday.'

I stayed at home baking cupcakes. And then ate them all while watching a documentary about handsome engineers building a tunnel. 'We just had some drinks and a bite to eat,' she says, wincing through the lie. 'It was… fine.'

'And do you think you'll see him again?'

Alice looks out at the rolling farmland, the emotional safety of London feeling far removed. 'Yes, I'd like to,' she says, certain that if she had been on a date last night, that's how she'd be feeling right now.

'And he feels the same way?' replies Rachel, the merest hint of disbelief in her voice.

'Yes,' she says, swallowing her indignation, but that one word feels like an insufficient response. 'He's very enthusiastic, in fact. I get the feeling that we'll see a lot more of each other.'

46 minutes later, Wickford, Essex

By the time she's walking up the front path of her parents' house, she can't even remember why she thought this was a good idea; is wondering if she could still quietly sneak away when the front door opens.

'Darling, how are you?' says her mother, pulling her into the same hug as always, less an embrace than a physical inspection; her hand lingering a moment too long on Alice's waistline. 'It feels like you've gained a few pounds.'

'I'm really not sure,' replies Alice, hoping to sound clueless rather than a liar.

Her mother leads her through to the kitchen, a fragrant wonderland of bubbling pots and roasting meat. 'It's not diet food, but you can just eat less of it, can't you?'

'Is Dad upstairs?'

'Where else? Playing with his toy trains, as usual.'

Alice thinks of pointing out that he's not *playing*, he's creating an elaborate parallel reality – though this probably isn't what her mother wants to hear, given that he's only doing it because he dislikes their shared reality so much. 'I'm sure he'll be down soon,' is all she says.

'I don't want to talk about him, I want to hear about you. Tell me things.'

'Well, I'm thinking I might look for somewhere else to live. Mei's becoming a bit of a handful.'

'That's the thing, isn't it? The Chinese are taking over the world. You can run, but you can't hide. And how's your love life?'

'Like I've said before, work is keeping me so busy, I just want to focus on my career for now.'

'It's such a shame you get your metabolism from your father's side of the family. When I was your age, I was having to beat the boys away with a brickbat.' She gives her daughter a pitying look. 'I worry about you, that's all. My poor, poor

36

little Alice. If you can't have some fun at your age, you never will.'

'Actually,' says Alice, the words tripping out with a surprising ease, 'there is someone. His name's Ben.'

In the silence that follows, her mother primps her hair, as if the thought of Alice dating someone has just made her feel a little less beautiful. 'And why haven't we heard of Ben before?'

'We, er, well, we've not known each other for long, and we both want to take things slowly. Like I said, I'm really focused on my job at the moment.'

'But don't be too slow, darling. Men are easily bored.' Another careful rearrangement of hair and blouse. 'And what does Ben do?'

'He's, er… he's an engineer. A civil engineer.'

'Lovely,' she replies, clearly unsure what that is. 'We all like a civil man. Of course, the big question is, when are we going to meet him?'

'I think it's a little early for that.'

'We're not getting any younger.'

'You're only sixty. Even Dad is, what? Sixty-five?'

'But when you think of all the tension that I have to live with on a daily basis…' She stares at the ceiling, as though X-ray vision enables her to see Alice's father in plain sight, doubtless doing something that irritates her. 'I sometimes think that's why he keeps himself so busy up there, tinkering and playing with his toys: he's trying to drive me to an early grave.'

*

Alice eventually joins her father in the attic, finds him tending to his vast model train layout as usual: dusting mountaintops with snow; doting over his creations like some benevolent God.

'Alice,' he says, glancing up from his work. 'Have you been here long?'

'Long enough. I've come seeking refuge.'

'Well, you've come to the right place. It's almost like your mother is a mosquito. She never climbs to this altitude.'

'I just wonder if she doesn't feel a bit lonely with you up here all the time.'

'I'm afraid that's the thing about being a passive-aggressive bitch. One tends to end up lonely.' He steps back to admire his handiwork: an Alpine wonderland rich with the promise of wintry pleasures. 'If it's any consolation, I'm sure I can convince her to have some wine with lunch.'

'She probably wouldn't drink at all if you didn't encourage her.'

'But it does work a treat in softening her edges.'

'A little too much, to be honest. How are the two of you getting on these days?'

'Let's just say, if it was a game of chess, it would be stalemate.'

'There must be something you can do about that. It sounds so defeatist.'

'One day you'll understand,' he says, his tone as matter-of-fact as always. 'Over the years, a couple grows to hate one another. It's just nature's way.'

*

As usual, Alice's mother seats her at the dining table with a clear view of her school photos, the largest of which is a picture of her during an awkward phase at the age of twelve, a chunky dental brace appearing to be in a life-and-death struggle with her teeth. She's just started wondering if her parents only keep it to make sure that she never wants to move back in, when her father speaks: 'The two of you have barely touched your wine,' he says, his glass almost empty.

'Is that a crime?' replies Alice's mother.

'Not at all, but I would like to propose a toast.' He raises his glass to her. 'Here's to your lovely food and the pleasures of a proper family lunch.'

'Thank you,' she says, picking up her glass of wine. 'It's always nice to be appreciated.' She takes a polite sip, has barely put her glass down when Alice's father is proposing another toast.

'And to Alice, not only for joining us today, but also for the future, for her exciting new life in London.'

'It's really not as exciting as you think,' says Alice.

'But it's early days,' he replies. 'What matters is that you're on your way.'

They all drink to this, even though Alice still isn't convinced that it's true. It's this second mouthful of wine that seems to push her mother over some invisible threshold.

'Ooh,' she says, looking at her glass of wine like she now sees in it something that wasn't there before. 'That's rather lovely, isn't it?' And now a bigger sip, her whole manner appearing to deflate. 'Yes, that's *very* nice.' She gestures at the table, laid with enough food for twice as many people. 'Everyone eat up,' she says, more motherly than she was just moments ago. 'Lord knows there's more than enough to go around.'

'Speaking of food,' says Alice, 'I've just started volunteering at a soup kitchen. I plan to do it every Sunday.'

'Oh, Alice,' replies her mother, drinking more wine. 'Why would you want to do something like that?'

'Because there are people out there who need help.'

'Why don't you volunteer with an animal charity instead? You know, kittens or elephants or something. There's no hidden agenda with animals.'

'Mother, these are young families, and the elderly, and… and people like us. No one has an agenda, other than not wanting to be hungry.'

'I just don't like the idea that someone may try to take advantage of your good nature. That would never happen with a hippo.' She appears to consider the statement. 'Wouldn't it be lovely to have a hippo?' she says, to no one in particular. 'Is that even allowed? We could turn the back garden into a big mud bath and just watch him play all day.' Alice glances at her father, official acknowledgement that her mother has now gone into orbit; that by the time she's finished another glass or two, she'll be playing Il Divo too loudly, and will likely fall asleep on the sofa soon after. And still she's talking about the merits of getting a hippo. 'Tony would be a nice name, don't you think? Tony the hippo.'

'I'll drink to that,' says her husband, raising another toast. 'To Tony.'

'To Tony,' she replies, drinking yet more wine.

'And please,' he says, reaching over with the bottle, 'let me top you up.'

'Mother, I think you'll find that hippos are actually very dangerous animals.'

'Alice, it's that sort of naivety that makes me worry about you. You can't believe everything you read online.' She reaches over and puts her hand on Alice's, sounds more emotional. 'See, this is what it's like to be a mother. It's just *constant* worry. As if it's not enough that you're battling your weight. And now you've got Ben to think of too.'

'Who's Ben?' says Alice's father.

'Has she not told you? She's got a new man in her life. An engineer. A very civil one, by all accounts.'

'Alice,' he says, 'that's wonderful. I say we should drink to that.' He raises another toast, watches happily as Alice's mother drinks again. 'So, when are we going to meet him?'

'How did we get from a discussion of homelessness to hippos, and my love life?'

Her mother gives her hand a drunken squeeze. 'So you *do* have a love life, then? Are you using condoms?'

'Mother, I'm trying to talk about everything that's wrong with modern society.'

'Oh, please,' she replies. 'I understand the world just fine.'

Alice's father raises another toast. 'Here's to all the things we know.'

She drinks to that too, not even seeming to notice as he refills her glass.

'I just need to go and open another bottle,' he says, leaving the room.

Alice's mother leans across the table, her emotions now in complete surrender to alcohol. 'Poor sweet Alice,' she says. 'You're just so young. You probably don't even know about photocopiers getting jammed. Or those rolls of awful shiny paper we used to have in fax machines.'

'What's a fax machine?'

'See!'

'Mother, I was joking.'

'But *I'm* not. Look at me, I'm a relic from a former time.' She glances in the direction of the kitchen, Alice's father still out of sight. 'One moment you're dancing to a-ha and Rick Astley, the next you're married to a man who wears his socks to bed and plays with model trains.'

'Really, Mother, it's okay, you don't need to tell me any of this.'

'When I was your age, all I dreamt of was dating a man with a mobile phone. They were as big as a baby's arm in those days, but we all thought they were so sophisticated. Then I met your father…' She takes another mouthful of wine, does a bad job of trying to speak discreetly. 'I thought it was a good thing that the sex was disappointing. I just thought it was one less thing to go wrong later.'

Alice's father breezes back into the room, with a new bottle.

'No, thanks,' says Alice, as he moves to top up her glass.

He fills it up anyway. 'Alice, a glass of wine is like a napkin. You don't have to use it, but you can't sit at the table without one. It's a matter of etiquette.'

Alice's mother is still squeezing her hand, a faraway look in her eyes. 'The things I could tell you about the eighties. I had hair as big as my ambition. And it just makes me so sad to think that you haven't had any of those experiences.'

'Mother, I'm fine.'

'But let's face it, you're carrying more than a few extra pounds. And judging by the way it makes you look, it can't be by choice.' She stands up, her body beginning to sashay to some silent rhythm. 'I think we're ready for a bit of Il Divo, don't you?'

'Not really,' replies Alice, but her mother is already fumbling with a remote control. Moments later, the opening bars of 'Unbreak My Heart' begin to boom across the room.

Dancing now, her mother gestures at the table. 'I'll pack up some of the food later. You can give it to Ben.'

'You've never offered to give me food before.'

'Oh, darling, of course not. Someone like you needs a gym membership, not a doggy bag.'

The No.2 bus towards Marylebone Station

¾ mile from Alice

It was Hyde Park that did it. Until then, the bus ride had been uneventful, Ben spending most of the journey thinking about some of the TV commercials he'd seen at the weekend: how much he'd like his own life to be bonfires on the beach, and well-behaved dogs, and soft clothes in neutral colours.

It's as his bus rounds Hyde Park Corner, turning left up Park Lane, that he sees Alice, standing beneath a tree on the edge of the park, her yellow dress appearing to glow in the morning sun. She waves to him as if she'd always known that he'd be on that precise bus, sitting right there in a window seat on the upper deck. As Ben sails past, he thinks of getting off at the next stop, of going back to find her, but then he's passing her again, on a bench this time, sitting right there by the side of the road, eating a large ice cream. Ben waves at her, so distracted that he thinks aloud. 'She's mad to be eating ice cream in this weather. As mad as chicken nuggets.' He doesn't notice how the people sitting near him begin to shift in their seats, doubtless wondering whether they should be worried.

A minute or two later the bus is snared in traffic near Marble Arch and Alice again comes into view, this time passing him on a bicycle, her yellow dress billowing in the wind. Ben starts to laugh, the two of them waving to each other even as she turns westward, growing smaller and smaller as she heads out across the park.

15 minutes later, Oxford Street, London W1
500 yards from Alice

To look at everyone else at work, anyone would think this is just another day: the same faces eating the same muffins from the same place as always; wearing clothes that Ben's seen countless times before. If it wasn't for Alice this morning, he isn't even sure how he'd recognize this as a new day rather than the mere replay of any one of hundreds of other days just like it.

He's still standing in the middle of the stockroom, shocked that he's never noticed any of this before, when his boss, Hilary, approaches. 'Good morning, Ben. Did you have a nice weekend?'

He stares at her, the sense of déjà vu growing stronger by the second. 'That's what you always ask me. Every Monday. Every week, always the same.'

She looks unsure how to respond, clearly decides to press on with the conversation anyway. 'I had a lovely weekend, but it was—'

'Too short.'

In the silence that follows, her smile begins to look more forced. 'I was wondering if we could have a little chat in my office? Nothing to worry about. Just a chance to catch up.'

He follows her through to her private domain, the desk suggestive of someone with a high threshold for clutter. 'This place is almost as bad as my flat,' says Ben. 'I bet your house is a right mess.' Sensing that this may not have been a diplomatic thing to say, he speaks again. 'You're looking particularly haggard today. I hope it's not my fault.'

It takes her a moment to reply. 'Why would it be your fault?'

'Because I can be, you know, hard work.' He casts his mind back to what his psychiatrist used to say. '"Not everyone has the necessary patience".'

'I'd like to think I do.'

46

'Definitely. You're great at that.' He notices how the words seem to breathe new life into her, so that for a moment her skin appears a little less lacklustre, her hair a little less limp.

'I don't want you worrying about me,' she says, blushing, as though no one has worried about her for years. 'And there's no need to worry about this chat, either. I just think, after last week's little incident where you didn't come back after lunch…'

'Yeah, sorry about that. Like I told you, I, er, forgot.'

'I was thinking we could play a game. I'd like you to think of someone you admire for their work ethic. Someone whom you think works really hard.'

'Brad Pitt,' he replies, in an instant.

'Well, it doesn't have to be the first person you think of.' She waits, perhaps hoping that silence will prompt Ben to sprout new ideas. 'I'm sure Mr Pitt works very hard,' she says, finally, 'but maybe you could think of people more like you and me. In fact, maybe it's even better if it's not an actual person, more a *type* of person. Like a baker, perhaps; someone who gets up very early every day. Or a postman, delivering letters in all weathers. The idea is that we can identify role models. People that we can imitate here at work.'

'In that case,' he says, dragging the words out while he racks his brain for a new answer, 'I'd have to say… the peasants in the French Revolution. I mean, you've got to hand it to them, they were very thorough.'

She stares at her hands, seems unsure what to say next. 'Maybe we should just forget the game. I think we should talk about how you're getting on at work. Are you still enjoying your job?'

'It's funny you ask, because I was thinking on the bus this morning that I should quit today.'

'Quit?'

47

'Yes. In fact, if you don't mind, I should probably leave now.'

'I think we should talk about it first. Maybe there's something I can do to make things better.'

Ben pictures Alice again in Hyde Park, waving to him as she rode off into the distance; not a goodbye at all, but an *invitation*. 'Actually,' he says, 'I've decided to leave London.'

'You're moving away?'

'Yeah, that's right.' He smiles at the thought, the plan suddenly feeling real and achievable. 'So if you don't mind, I should go home and pack.'

Mayfair, London W1

Monday mornings mean only one thing in Alice's world: the agency's weekly team meeting; an opportunity for people who hate each other to sit in a claustrophobic room and vent their aggression. Geneva was already in a difficult mood when she got to the office – every look, every sigh, suggestive of murderous intentions – but as Piers announces that they have a new client, things rapidly become much, much worse.

He puts five plastic bottles on the table, each containing lurid goo in neon shades. 'You're about to fall in love with these condiments.'

'Why on earth would you assume that?' says Geneva.

Piers ignores her. 'They're already available at selected retailers. They're visionary, they're exciting, and we're going to give them a glitzy launch that makes them bigger than God.'

Geneva stares at the bottles. 'They're exactly how I imagine radioactive waste.'

Piers turns to Alice, gives her such a disarming smile she feels her heart skip a beat. 'Alice, I would like you to prepare the media pack. Under Geneva's guidance, of course.'

By now, Geneva is holding one of the bottles, her expression a picture of disgust. 'You could get cancer just looking at it.'

'There's just one small challenge,' says Piers to the whole table. 'The client wants a major event. Some famous faces, the whole nine yards.' He pauses, everyone hanging on his words. 'And they want it in three weeks' time.'

'For Christ's sake,' says Geneva, 'we practise PR, not miracles. This meeting is adjourned.' She gets up, heads for the door. 'Really, Piers, I think you shouldn't even open your mouth unless you have something sensible to say.'

She's barely left the room when everyone else starts getting up too, the meeting beginning to feel more like a plane that's disintegrated in mid-flight.

Alice remains at the table, the only one who does.

'It's nothing I didn't anticipate,' says Piers, with a smile. 'She'll come around.'

*

'Have you ever heard anything so preposterous?' says Geneva, when Alice returns to her desk. 'As if the products alone aren't hideous enough.'

'Three weeks is a bit tight, isn't it?'

'Let me put it this way. It's like asking an agency to turn you into a swimwear model by the end of the month. Only a madman would even think it possible.'

Piers swoops in, shouting to Geneva across Alice. 'Pray tell, Geneva, what precisely is it that you have against this client?'

'Forgive me for not wanting to take it up the arse from a ketchup manufacturer.'

'They may lack breeding, but I can assure you that they are filthy rich.'

'It sounds like you have so much in common, I'm surprised you even need my help.'

'Geneva, our job—'

'Please don't use that word. It's horribly sordid.'

'Fine, our *renown* is based on making things happen, not on

49

liking our clients. We both know that this whole problem could be solved if you simply *made a phone call.*'

There's an odd moment of silence, like he's just said something in code.

'You're right that I *could*,' she says, glancing at Alice as she says it. 'But as you know, I prefer to keep my powder dry.'

'Well, too bad,' he bellows back at her. 'Heavy rain is forecast and we're going into battle anyway.'

By now, Alice's desk feels more like a no man's land, artillery whistling overhead. She scoops Harry from the floor. 'He looks like he needs a walk.'

'He was sleeping,' says Geneva.

'Don't worry,' replies Alice, already rushing for the door, 'we'll be back in a little while.'

*

Short of running from the building, Alice gets away from the office as quickly as possible, carrying Harry through the streets of Mayfair lest he slow her down. Grosvenor Square Garden is just coming into sight when she hears Piers's voice. 'Alice, hold on.' He catches up with her, breathless. 'I'd like to join you, if you don't mind. I could do with some fresh air.' He lights a cigar as they walk. 'Sorry about all the drama back there. Working with Geneva sometimes requires a firm hand.'

'Not a luxury I can afford.'

'I wouldn't say that. You handle her very well.'

'I think you'll find she's the handler; I'm just the docile *handlee*. I'm basically Harry, but without the metabolism.'

They walk in silence, every puff of his cigar seeming to make Piers more relaxed. 'Just for the record, I know she calls me Glasgow, and I want you to know that I don't care one bit.'

'I'd much rather be named after a place of hard-working men and women than a city of tax dodgers and looted Jewish gold.'

'Brava! I couldn't have said it better myself.' He takes another puff on his cigar, sighs happily. 'It's so refreshing to have you around, Alice. You're not like the others at all.'

'As they like to remind me. On a daily basis.'

'But I mean it in a good way. It's precisely why I wanted you in the agency. You're hungry for it, and you'll work for it, I can see that. Unlike the rest of those gilded wankers, everyone assuming they're entitled to be successful because their parents have a chalet in Klosters.'

'You were the one who hired them.'

'Touché. Sometimes we have to work with the system, as imperfect as it is.'

'Though let's be honest, they're not *bad* people.' She sees his disbelief. 'Not once you've got used to them.' And still he looks unconvinced. 'Maybe what I'm trying to say is, at least they're not *evil*. Not in a conscious, premeditated way.'

'See, this is my point,' he says. 'You're the kind of person we need. Someone who can always find the positive, against all the odds. God knows, it's an important skill in this business.'

As they enter the garden, Alice puts Harry down; watches as he takes his first tentative steps on the grass, his manner suggesting that he doesn't much like the outdoors.

'If only we worked in the wilds of Africa,' says Piers. 'Imagine the pleasure of seeing him snatched by a leopard or a massive bird of prey.'

'I'm sure you don't mean that,' she says.

'I'll remind you of that next time he throws up in the office.' He checks his watch. 'Look, I should be getting back.'

'Sure, we'll just, you know...' She gestures at the garden. *Stay here for as long as possible. Stay here for ever.*

'Don't worry about Geneva. Everything will be fine by this afternoon. I already know she'll do exactly what I want.'

'What did she mean about keeping her powder dry?'

He waves his cigar dismissively. 'It's not important. What matters is that the storm has broken. It'll be clear skies from here on.' He starts walking away, but then stops and calls to her. 'I just want you to know, Alice, I'm watching out for you in the office. I know Geneva can be hard work, but you and I, I think we could be good allies.'

He stands there, clearly waiting for a reply.

'I'd like that too,' says Alice, trying not to blush. 'I really would.'

The No.2 bus towards Norwood
3½ miles from Alice

Ben can't decide if it's a good or a bad thing that there's no sign of Alice on the bus journey home. Given that he's just quit his job in order to be with her, he'd imagined that she would be waving to him from every corner; that the bus may, in fact, travel back to south London in a three-mile ticker tape parade, Ben riding on the upper deck while the whole city celebrates his new-found love. With most people still travelling in the opposite direction, his bus grows emptier in direct correlation to the streets becoming quieter and dirtier. Twenty minutes after crossing the Thames, he's one of the only passengers left on board, and the final walk home through silent streets only heightens the feeling that he has somehow lost his grip on reality; that life is now something that only happens to other people in some other place.

It's the bicycle bell he hears first, echoing down the street of grey brick terraces; too playful, too happy, to be one of the usual cyclists round here. As he turns to look, he doesn't see Alice so much as glimpse something: a yellow blur passing the end of the street.

'Wait,' he shouts, certain that it's her. 'Alice, wait!' He sprints to the corner, only to find that she's already a hundred yards off. 'Alice!'

She turns in a graceful arc, her broad smile coming back towards him like the white crest on a wave of yellow.

'Riding a bike is so much fun,' she calls to him, as she gets closer. 'Do you like bicycles?'

'I can't remember. It's been a long time.'

'I love cycling and so will you. It's like flying.' She loops around him, first once and then again. 'Once you start, you'll never want to stop.' Laughing, she begins to ride away. 'You'll want to cycle from here to the moon and back.'

'But I don't want to go to the moon.'

'Then wherever your heart desires,' she shouts, getting further and further away. 'Remember, Ben, you must always follow your heart. Always.'

*

The living room curtains are still shut when Ben gets home, a sure sign that Dave is working on more candles, the whole flat doubtless smelling like toothpaste or molten candy or weaponized vanilla. As he opens the front door, he's engulfed in a cloud of cinnamon so strong, it's almost a physical assault.

'Ben?' shouts Dave, from the living room. 'Why aren't you at work?'

'What would you think if I cycled to—' He reaches the living room to find Dave at work with their friend, Agnes. 'What are you doing here?'

'And hello to you too,' she replies, barely glancing up at him while she arranges dried leaves in candle moulds.

'Agnes is helping me with some new ideas,' says Dave.

Ben sits opposite them. 'One day you'll find yourself a husband,' he says to Agnes. 'Presumably someone old and blind, and then you'll leave us in peace.'

'So,' says Dave, 'why aren't you at work?'

'That's what I'm trying to ask you. What do you think if I cycled to Glasgow?'

'One, I'd think you were mad, and two, I'd think you were likely to die on the way.'

'Dave, I'm serious.'

'So am I. And now I'm worried what this has to do with being home from work early.'

'I quit.'

'Ben! You can't do that.'

'I obviously can, because I did.'

'What I'm trying to say is, it's a mistake. It's absolutely the worst decision you could have made.'

'It's funny you say that because I was beginning to think the same thing on the way home, but then...' *I saw Alice. She told me to start cycling.* 'Let's just say, I had a change of heart.'

'Ben, call your boss now and tell her you didn't mean it.'

'But I did. I'm going to Glasgow. By bike.'

'And what about money?'

'I've got a few hundred in the bank. Cycling doesn't cost anything, so all I need is some cash for a cheap B&B and the odd bag of chips.' Dave shakes his head, clearly lost for words. 'You can't tell me it's not normal.'

'Ben, we've had this discussion many times. There's no such thing as "normal". The question is simply whether it's *advisable*.'

'But you're the one who's always telling me that I can do anything in life. Despite, you know, my *problems*.'

'And I mean it, Ben, you can.'

'Fine, then I'm going to Scotland.'

'It's a long way,' says Agnes.

'How far, do you reckon?' replies Ben.

'I don't know, four hundred miles, maybe.'

'That's not *so* far, is it? If I ride at about...' He does the

54

maths on his fingers. 'If I ride at a steady twenty miles an hour, I can get up there in a day.'

'I think,' says Dave, with a sigh, 'you'll need to revise that calculation.'

'And what happens when you get there?' says Agnes. 'How are you going to find this woman?'

'I'll Google it or something.'

'You're just going to Google "Alice" and "Glasgow"?'

'You'd be surprised how many results that brings up. Anyway, cycling all the way up there is the kind of thing that will get me noticed, isn't it? It'll get me in the newspapers, maybe even on TV.'

'Only if you're doing it for charity,' she replies.

'Fine, I'll do it for charity.'

'As a total afterthought. That's very noble of you.'

'All that matters is I get noticed. Alice will see me on the news and she'll get in touch, I know she will.'

'Just for the record,' says Dave. 'You don't "know" that.'

But I do. She almost said as much, just now, out in the street. Ben swallows the words, certain that honesty would not be helpful at this precise moment. 'So, Agnes,' he says, giving her his sweetest smile. 'How about you lend me your bike?'

'Piss off.'

'Please.'

'Even if you didn't spend most of your time insulting me, how do you think *I* get around?'

Ben is about to say on a broomstick, but then decides that this would probably be the wrong strategy. 'Everything I say to you, it's all banter, you know that.' She looks unconvinced. 'You're a...' He forces himself to say it. 'You're a lovely girl and, er, one day a man will feel very lucky to have you. And that's "have" in the married sense, not just some bloke knocking you up in the toilets.'

'The answer's still no,' she replies. 'But Dave has a bike.'

'Don't encourage him,' says Dave.

'You're not talking about that fold-up thing, are you?' says Ben, disgusted.

'It's still a bike,' replies Dave, sounding offended now.

'Hardly,' says Ben. 'But thanks for the offer. I'll consider it.'

'I didn't offer. This whole idea is madness.' He turns to Agnes. 'You're going to stop encouraging him. And,' he turns back to Ben, 'you're going to forget this crazy, ill-advised scheme, and ask for your job back.'

Ben pictures Alice pedalling away, telling him to follow his heart. 'If I do make this trip—'

'Oh, God,' says Dave. 'I swear, once you get an idea in your head, you're like a dog with a bone. When was the last time you even rode a bike?'

'Mate, you're totally over-thinking this.' And still Dave looks concerned. 'Basically, I just cycle north for a day or two. How hard can that be?'

Mayfair, London W1

It's only when Alice gets to the office that she discovers both Geneva and Piers are away this morning, the rest of her colleagues clearly assuming that this negates the need for work of any kind. To look at Lucy – already sloth-like and disinterested – it's obvious that in another hour or two the whole office will resemble a rock pool at low tide: slimy, mollusc-like creatures stranded at their desks, near-lifeless. Not wanting to be like them, Alice dedicates her morning to other pleasures: the office's expensive coffee machine, for instance, which normally feels like a consolation prize – *Yes, we know your life sucks, but here, have a cappuccino* – today is her private barista, a sexy Italian offering her as much coffee as she wants, all of which can be enjoyed without Geneva lecturing her about the perils of caffeine and the fattening effects of milk. For the first time since starting this job, she can also freely experiment with the pneumatic, reclining and swivel functions of her overpriced ergonomic chair, rocking and spinning and bouncing her way through the morning.

She's on her fourth coffee – wide-eyed and a little jittery – when she starts to write a list; nay, a manifesto.

Things I can accomplish with my new ally Piers:

1. **Fire everyone and start a new agency.**

2. **Bury Geneva in a shallow grave.**

Feeling guilty now, she tries to cross the words out, but they seem immune to deletion, still legible on the page as if they're taking on a life of their own. She crosses through them again and again, pressing so hard that she tears the page to shreds.

'Alice, what are you doing?'

She looks up to find Geneva standing right there behind her, the caffeine in Alice's bloodstream giving the whole experience an ominous quality. 'I was making notes,' she says. 'About the launch party. You know, er, brain-storming.'

Geneva glances at the ink-smudged shreds of paper in front of her. 'I'm happy to announce that everything is sorted for the party now, so thankfully we only need you for the grunt work, not your creative genius.' She retreats to her desk. 'Our guest of honour will be Suzie Franklin.'

Alice gasps. '*The* Suzie Franklin?'

'The one and only. Model, TV presenter, It girl, blah, blah, blah…'

'How did you manage that?'

'Oh, it was nothing. I just made a phone call or two.'

'Suzie Franklin,' says Alice, still in awe. 'I was watching her on TV the other night.'

'She's everywhere at the moment. You could probably lift a rock in the park and find her.'

'And yet we got her at such short notice?'

'*I* got her,' she replies, the words sounding unexpectedly harsh. She softens her tone, but there's still something cruel in her smile. 'It turns out that Suzie loves the client's products. She and her family already use them every day. Imagine the serendipity.'

'Is Piers with the client now?'

'Haven't you heard? We'll be working south of the border for the next few days.' She appears to gloat over the words, then realizes that Alice hasn't understood. 'He's sick. Sick as a half-breed mutt. So sick, in fact, I doubt he'll be in for the rest of the week.'

'Oh no,' says Alice, already wondering how she can get his address; what she can take him that will strengthen their bond.

'Food poisoning,' says Geneva. 'He ate some dodgy oysters.'

'Does he have anyone to look after him?'

'Oh, please, who cares? It's all his own fault. If only he'd stuck to his roots, to fish and chips, perhaps, or a kebab, none of this would have happened. His real problem wasn't a bad oyster, it was hubris.'

Beckenham, South London
9½ miles from Alice

'When I decided to give your bike a try,' says Ben, 'I didn't think it would involve this.' He watches as Dave searches through the dusty, accumulated junk of his mother's garage. 'I always thought your mum was more organized.'

'Ben, everyone's garage looks like this.' He peers inside another box, coughing on the dust. 'I think you'll find it's an established fact that only sociopaths have neat and tidy garages.'

'You can't find it, can you? This is the problem with a toy bike.'

'It's a *folding* bike, not a toy bike.'

'My point being that at least you can find a proper bike.'

'It *is* a proper bike, Ben, it's just a *folding* bike.' He starts moving other boxes. 'It's in here somewhere, I know it.'

Having already heard that statement countless times this morning, Ben wanders to the open garage door, stands there watching the rain. Behind him, Dave is still heaving boxes around, still talking to himself. 'If ever you see a neat and tidy garage, I suggest you run as fast as you can, because the owners are sure to be certifiable axe murderers.' There's a loud crash, as an entire stack of boxes tumbles over. Ben turns, expecting the worst, but Dave stands there in a grey cloud, looking pleased with himself. 'Bingo!' he says, lifting up a geometric tangle of metal.

'What am I supposed to do with *that*? It's not a bike, it's origami.'

'Ben, you were the one demanding to see it. I'm perfectly happy to just put it away and go home.'

'No, no, I mean, we're here, right? I may as well give it a chance.'

'It's actually very easy to put together,' says Dave, as he begins assembling it. 'It's great for taking on the train too.'

Ben watches as he locks it into shape piece by piece. 'It's like the IKEA of bikes, isn't it? You'll probably find a bit's missing in a moment, then you'll be screwed.'

'Trust me, everything you need is right here.' Dave keeps working, the bike appearing less and less abstract by the second. 'And hey presto!'

Ben stares at it, underwhelmed. 'No wonder you don't use it. It's not really a bike, is it? It's basically just a way of saying to the world "Hate me, I'm a wanker".'

'Fine,' says Dave, already beginning to dismantle it. 'Be like that.'

Out in the street, the sound of a bicycle bell. Ben turns to find Alice at the bottom of the driveway, sitting on her bicycle in the rain, smiling at him beneath a big yellow umbrella.

'You know what?' says Ben. 'I think I will take it for a spin.'

'You just said you hated everything about it.'

'Yeah, well, I'm, er, open to being wrong, aren't I?'

'Since when? And it's raining.'

Out on the street, Alice rings her bell again and pedals away.

'It's only water,' says Ben, taking the bike from Dave and hurrying towards the driveway.

Dave plucks an old golf umbrella from another box. 'At least take this,' he says. He watches as Ben inches into the rain, trying to balance both the bike and the umbrella. 'You do know that you could just wait for the rain to stop.'

'Mate, this is England. We could be here for days.'

He pushes off down the driveway, accelerating faster than expected.

'Look out for cars,' yells Dave, as Ben zooms into the street.

'I'll be fine,' he shouts, already turning out of sight. Up ahead, Alice is gently pedalling along the street, her umbrella so perfectly poised it appears that she may float away at any second. Tilting his umbrella into the wind, Ben pedals harder. 'Alice,' he says, 'wait for me.'

When he finally pulls alongside, she gives him a big smile. 'See, this is fun, isn't it?' she says.

'I could do without the rain.'

'But think of the ducks and the trees. They must be thrilled with it. They're probably singing to themselves right now. We could sing along with them, if you want.'

'You're as mad as I am.'

'Ben, there's nothing mad about having joy in your heart. People would be much happier if they started each day by saying "Hello, Mister Sunshine!"'

Ben tries to keep pace with her, but his umbrella and the gusts of wind make everything more complicated. 'This is much harder than I thought,' he says, as she pulls ahead.

'It just takes practice,' she calls back. Ben comes to a stop, watches as she cycles further and further down the street. 'It's like everything in life,' she says, her voice already growing faint. 'Practice makes perfect.'

*

Dave is still sheltering beneath the garage door when Ben returns. 'What happened?' he says, as Ben pushes the bike up the driveway.

'You know how you said this bike would be convenient for taking the train?'

'Yeah.'

63

'Well, I'm thinking maybe that's an even better idea. That I just take the train to Scotland.'

'I thought you'd decided to do this for charity?'

'I still can.'

'But it's not a very compelling proposition, is it? Sponsoring you to sit on a train for six hours.'

'I can't ride this bloody thing to Scotland. I can barely ride it around the block.'

'And as far as I'm concerned that's a good thing. I don't want you cycling to Scotland.' He returns the bike to a dusty corner. 'Now we can just forget all about it.'

Mayfair, London W1

By three o'clock in the afternoon, the office is so quiet Alice can hear her own breathing. Geneva sits at her desk, ostensibly working, but it's obvious that she's watching and listening to everyone else, spider-like, the entire room her web.

And then Alice's phone rings.

'Hello?' she says, aware that Geneva is surely following every word.

'Alice, it's me, your mother.'

'I'm busy right now.'

'Then I won't hold you up. I'm just calling to say your father's away this weekend. Some exhibition or other about model trains.' Silence now, presumably an invitation to dialogue. 'I thought we could spend some time together. It will be so much nicer without him.'

'I can't,' says Alice, wanting to keep every statement as short as possible.

'But why?'

Because you always make me feel bad. Because we don't do mother–daughter stuff. We never have. 'I just can't.'

'At least give me a good reason.'

'I'm busy.'

'We're all busy, Alice.'

She lowers her voice. 'I have a date.'

'Why are you whispering?'

'I'm not.'

'I can barely hear you.'

Louder now. 'I said, I have a date.'

'Oh, of course, with the engineer. What's his name again?'

'Ben,' she says, quietly.

'Alice, would you please stop doing that? I can't hear a word you're saying.'

'Ben,' she says, louder.

'Well, why don't you both come down for the weekend? I'll cook.'

'Sorry, I need to go now,' says Alice, already picturing the cruel smile on Geneva's face.

'Well, let me know if you change your mind about the weekend.'

'I won't. Change my mind, I mean. Bye.'

She's barely put the phone down when Geneva speaks. 'So who's Ben?'

'No one.'

'But you're dating?'

'Well, you know…'

'Alice, there's no need to be shy about it. I think it's wonderful that you've found someone. And he obviously doesn't mind a few extra pounds on a girl.'

'He likes it, in fact. He encourages me to eat whatever I want.'

'And for someone like you, that's surely the very definition of a keeper. Though with a man in your life, you're going to have to reconsider your wardrobe.'

Alice looks down at her yellow dress. 'Don't you like it? It's new.'

'Don't tell me, it was on sale. There's a reason that clothes like that are sold at half-price. You were wearing it last week and it looked no better than it does now.'

Alice's heart sinks. Until a few seconds ago, she'd thought of this dress as a sunbeam of sorts; had pictured herself as a ray of light in a dark place. 'Do you really not like it?'

'It's how I imagine a funerary shroud in some god-awful one-horse town. The colour ages you terribly. And it adds at least ten pounds, as if that's possible.' She starts tapping at her keyboard. 'Speaking of which, would you take Harry for a walk? You could probably both do with the exercise.'

★

It doesn't matter that it's raining. At least the park is quiet, and there's no chance that Geneva may appear at any moment, criticizing her posture, or telling her that her teeth are crooked, or her coat looks cheap.

Although Harry has been on the ground for several minutes, he's spent the entire time pressed against Alice's leg, trying to shelter beneath her umbrella.

'Harry, this is not the point of being a dog. You're supposed to be running around, getting wet and muddy.' Trembling now, he looks up at her with such imploring eyes she actually pities him, this dog whose collection of cashmere sweaters and tweed capes is probably worth more than her entire wardrobe. 'Fine,' she says, scooping him up. 'I'll do the walking.'

It's only when she reaches the bench where she met Ben that she thinks of him; realizes that she was wearing the same dress that day, evidently looking even worse than she'd imagined. Still, as she stands there in the rain, she tries to savour the memory: how his smile managed to light up her day; how, for a brief moment at least, the world seemed a better, kinder place.

Richmond, South West London

It wasn't a hard decision to take the day off sick. After leaving a message on Geneva's voicemail, doing her best to sound dangerously bacterial, Alice tells herself that if sickness can be defined as a loss of oomph then she *is* sick: her ability to skip into work and always look on the bright side is currently tucked up in bed, sweating out a fever.

'It felt like the right thing to do at the time,' she explains to Rachel, the two of them sitting outside a cafe. 'But now I just feel guilty.'

'I wouldn't give it a second thought,' replies Rachel.

'Says the person who doesn't have a job.' She watches Rachel toss buttery flakes of croissant to waiting sparrows, their numbers swelling by the second. 'I've never skipped work before. It feels like the start of a slippery slope.' Rachel says nothing, is too busy feeding the birds. Spotting a frail sparrow on the edge of the group, Alice tries to throw some of her own croissant, but the other birds get there first in a frantic scrum. 'That's not fair.'

'Life isn't,' replies Rachel, her tone suggesting that her singing ambitions have suffered another setback. Preferring not to have that conversation, Alice reaches out to a particularly emboldened sparrow, so close to them now that she can see the colour of its eyes.

'Not that one,' says Rachel. 'It looks like it has an arch personality.'

'Rachel, it's a bird.'

'Yeah, but look at its expression. You can just tell it's a bit evil.' They watch as another one inches closer. 'And don't give anything to that one. It looks like my mother.'

'Would you like to talk about that?'

Rachel sighs. 'She told me this morning that she expects me to get a job, any job.'

Alice tries to choose her response wisely. 'A job would give you financial independence, which would make it easier to, you know…' She tries to say *become a singer*, but can't get the words past her lips.

'She also said that I have to pay them back everything I've borrowed in the last twelve months.'

'Ouch.'

'My first thought was that I should just get on a plane to Los Angeles and try my luck, but to be honest it's got to the stage where I don't think they'd even lend me the money for the flight.'

Alice tosses the last of her crumbs to the waiting sparrows. 'You might enjoy working.'

'*You* don't.'

'That's not fair. It's getting better, slowly.'

'Alice, you've just called in sick because you hate it so much.'

'Only because Piers is away this week.' Rachel looks askance. 'I've told you about him,' she says, trying – and failing – to make it sound like no big deal. 'He's the guy who owns the agency.'

'And now you're what? Friends?'

'I wouldn't say friends. More like allies.'

'Alice, you're blushing.'

'I'm not.' She feels her cheeks redden. 'Okay, maybe I am, but only because it feels good to have someone on my side.'

'Is he attractive?'

'He's my boss.' Another blush. 'We're just friends.'

'You said you were allies just now.'

'Friendly allies. Allegiant friends.'

'You've only just started dating Ben…' A tense silence descends between them, the sparrows beginning to drift elsewhere. 'That's a bad sign, isn't it? Even the birds think we're boring.' The mood grows heavier. 'And they're probably right. This is turning into a bit of a shit day.'

'And I shouldn't have had that croissant. I'm feeling even fatter now.'

'Are you worried what Piers may think?' It's only as the last bird flies away that she speaks again. 'Sorry, I'm crap company today. The truth is, I got an email this morning. I've been offered a job.'

'That's great news. That's *amazing* news.' And yet still Rachel looks glum. 'Why didn't you say anything?'

'It's that trainee management programme I told you about.'

Alice wracks her brain, worried now that she may have dismissed some important nugget of information along with almost everything else that Rachel has said in recent months. 'Ah,' she says, finally, 'at the burger place.' She tries to summon an enthusiasm that even she doesn't feel. 'It's still a job. You'll be earning money.'

'And all the French fries I can eat.'

'I'd consider that a valuable perk.'

'But imagine the karma. Encouraging people to eat junk and die young just so I can afford a nice handbag.'

'We should do something to celebrate.'

'You're poor and I'm going to be in debt for years.'

'I don't care. This deserves to be celebrated. I'll think of something we can do this weekend. Just leave it to me, okay?'

Maidstone, Kent
38 miles from Alice

Ben's decision to make a spur-of-the-moment visit to his grand-parents is well intentioned, but it's clear that they're troubled by the spontaneity. His grandfather is as quiet as ever on the drive from the station, but this time his silence has a concerned quality too, as though Ben is about to break some terrible news. When they reach the house, it's evident that his grandmother is also expecting a dramatic revelation.

'I just want you to know,' she says, giving him a hug, 'that whatever you want to tell us, regardless of morality or accepted norms, we support you.'

'Gran, I'm only going to Scotland.'

'But that's the thing, you don't need to go away to be true to yourself.'

'No, it's—' He's cut short by the avian equivalent of an air-raid siren.

'Oh, I was in the middle of feeding Neville some pineapple,' she says, already hurrying away. 'The poor thing must be so confused.'

When Ben joins her in the living room, it becomes obvious that Neville may be feeling many emotions right now, but confusion is not one of them. After eyeing Ben with more than the usual hatred, he resumes chewing his pineapple.

'We're having spaghetti hoops for lunch,' says his grand-mother. Neville takes this opportunity to gloat in Ben's direction, sweet juice dripping from his beak. 'We bought a tin the other day and now we're addicted, aren't we, Frank?'

Ben turns to see if his grandfather adds anything to this discussion of haute cuisine, but he's already back in his usual armchair, holding the same book as always, his mind in a distant time and place.

'So, like I was saying,' says Ben, 'I'm going away.'

'No, no, Benjamin, save it for the dinner table. It's always nice to sort things out over food, don't you think?'

*

Ben can still remember, at the tender age of seven, asking his grandmother to buy a tin of spaghetti hoops. Back then, at the height of her mental powers, she was convinced that people only bought tinned food for major expeditions – to the Antarctic, say – or in anticipation of nuclear war, and yet seemed surprisingly unfazed that her local supermarket dedicated two entire aisles to these kinds of provisions. Instead, she'd insist on loading their trolley with cabbage, Brussels sprouts and anything else that was offensive and sulphurous, taking them all home and cooking them until they were better suited for spreading on bread.

So now, sixteen years later, there should be some sense of triumph that they are at last sitting down to a lunch of spaghetti hoops, lovingly spooned onto the plate without the frippery of being warmed up first. And yet there's also something sorrowful in these plates of shiny orange gloop; a reminder that the only real childhood this house has ever seen is his grandmother's slow regression into senility.

'There's no need to heat them up,' she explains, 'because they're already cooked. We don't want them turning to mush, do we?' She gives him the kind of carefree smile that can only come from having forgotten one's entire history.

'So, about my news,' says Ben. 'I'm going up to Glasgow to meet the girl I told you about.' He waits for some kind of response, but there's nothing: just two old people scooping up the crack cocaine of their tinned pasta. 'She's special. I think you'll like her.' Still nothing. 'I'll be able to introduce her to you soon. I'd love to bring her down here to meet you both.'

'We'd love that too,' replies his grandmother, in the same tone of voice she might use about meeting pixies at the bottom of the garden or flying to the moon with Tinker Bell.

'I was going to cycle up there, but—'

'Will you be going through the Peak District?' asks his grandfather. Fork frozen in mid-flight, Ben just stares at him, dumbstruck by this invitation to dialogue. 'If I was your age, I'd be making a beeline straight for those hills.'

'I'm not sure if the train goes through there.'

'That's why you need to do it on a bicycle. What a cracker of a ride it would be.'

And now Ben's grandmother is beaming at him too. 'How thrilling, Benjamin. It sounds like such an adventure.'

It sounds like a nightmare, thinks Ben. *Hills, bicycle, agony.* But the two of them are sitting in front of him, interested and engaged for the first time in decades, and Ben can't bear to disappoint them. 'I'll, er, look into it again. Maybe there's a way I can make that happen.'

'You must, you must,' says his grandfather, no indication that he's tiring of the subject. 'I only wish I could join you. Are you doing it for charity?'

'That was the original idea.'

'Oh, Benjamin,' says his grandmother, 'that's so laudable.'

'Yes,' adds his grandfather. 'It's a worthy thing, Benjamin, it really is.'

While he returns to the neon seduction of his lunch, Ben's grandmother sits there, smiling to herself. 'If only your parents were here to see it too. Little Benjamin, cycling to Scotland for charity. They'd be so proud of you.'

'Well, you know, it's still not completely decided,' says Ben. 'I might have to take the train for, you know, logistical reasons.'

'I'm sure you can figure it out,' she replies.

'And there's my, er, support team, of course. They've already said they're a bit worried about me. You know, being out on the road all alone.'

'Nonsense,' says his grandfather. 'You're a robust young man. You'll be fine.' He continues speaking even as he lifts mouthwards a trembling forkful of tinned pasta. 'I can't tell you how much I'm looking forward to hearing about the Peak District. And to seeing some pictures too. It'll be a real treat.'

Brixton, London SW2

13 miles from Alice

Even though Ben's been talking about Glasgow for a week already, Dave still appears shocked when Ben wakes him up and announces that he's leaving now, this minute.

'What do you mean, *now*?' he says, his voice still thick with sleep.

'I've got to go sooner or later.'

'But what about preparations and...' He looks at his clock, and groans. 'Mate, it's not even seven.'

'I thought it would be better to set off early, before the roads get too busy. I don't want to start riding in rush-hour traffic.'

Dave looks even more confused. 'Aren't you taking the train?'

'Um, no.' *I'm being emotionally blackmailed by my grandparents.* 'Let's just say, I changed my mind.'

'So where did you get a bike?'

'I'm using yours, of course. I went to your mum's place on the way home last night.'

'Thanks for telling me.'

'I didn't tell you. I swear you're getting as bad as my gran.'

'What happened to doing it for charity?'

'I'll figure something out on the way.'

'Ben,' he says, 'that's not how it works,' but Ben is already turning for the door. 'And what about all the other things you'll need, like maps?'

'I think you'll find Glasgow is signposted.'

'But probably not from here.'

'I just keep heading north, don't I?'

Dave scrambles out of bed. 'So that's it? You're just like, "Cheerio, I'm off to Scotland now"?'

'How am I supposed to say it?'

'I don't know, it just seems like a momentous occasion. I feel like I should give you a proper send off.'

'Well, I would give you a hug, but I'm not going near you without your clothes on.' They both look down at Dave's yellowing underpants, sagging around his crotch, a thick roll of belly fat spilling from above. 'You need a good woman in your life, but frankly I don't rate your chances.'

He picks up his backpack and heads for the front door.

'Wait,' says Dave, 'I'll come out too.' He hurriedly pulls on a trench coat and a pair of trainers, doesn't even tie the laces.

'Mate, now you just look creepy. Like the kind of bloke who hangs around a playground with pockets full of sweets.'

'What does it matter?' replies Dave. 'Everyone's still in bed.'

'For your sake, I hope that's true. For their sake too, actually.'

Once they're out on the street, Dave watches with some admiration as Ben assembles the bike. 'You're good at that.'

Ben locks the last piece into place. 'And now, if you'll give me a quick hug, I'll show you that I'm also good at pissing off.'

Dave pulls him into a bear hug, doesn't let go. 'You do know you don't have to do this, right?'

'But that's the thing, I do.'

'There are trains,' says Dave, still holding him tight.

'Mate, I can't breathe.'

'Sorry,' he replies, letting go. 'I just worry about you, you know that.'

'It's not that far. I was looking on a map last night. From here to Glasgow was only the width of four fingers.'

Dave bites his lip, is clearly holding back a response. 'Just be careful,' he says, finally. 'That's all I ask.'

*

For the first thirty or forty minutes, Ben can think only of Alice; constantly hoping that she'll pull alongside him on her bicycle, her smile as bright and cheerful as her yellow dress. The two of them will potter towards Central London together, perhaps while she sings happy songs or coos reassuringly about his cycling. It's the growing traffic that distracts him, the taxis and buses rushing by so close that he occasionally wobbles in their wake. By the time he nears Waterloo Station, there are other cyclists to contend with too, powering past him, their Lycra-clad thighs moving like the pistons of a finely tuned machine.

It's only as he crosses Westminster Bridge that it all begins to feel worthwhile; a sense that he isn't just cycling, he's *going places*. The Palace of Westminster sparkles in the morning sun, and Big Ben chimes eight o'clock as the bicycle carries him down into Parliament Square, the wheels humming happily beneath him. He follows the traffic towards Whitehall, past the Prime Minister's house and the soldiers standing motionless outside Horse Guards, only pausing to admire his surroundings as he enters Trafalgar Square. Standing there by the fountains, it's as though this ride has already taken on a magical quality: the rush-hour traffic revolving around him like a slow-motion tornado, beginning to lift him from his old life and carry him onwards to his personal Oz.

*

It's fair to say that everything went downhill from there. Yes, there was a certain pleasure in cycling up Charing Cross Road, seeing signs for places like Leicester Square and Covent Garden, but as the traffic grew thicker it seemed to Ben that he was really only moving from choke point to choke point. By the time he crossed the gridlocked traffic of the Inner Ring Road, there was no sense of magic, only a desire to get away from London as soon as possible. Resisting the lure of signs for Regent's Park and London Zoo, he kept heading north, progressing at a ceremonial pace into Camden, only to find the land rising up ahead of him, casting off the weight of the city. In search of flatter roads he veered right, heading deeper and deeper into Holloway, no longer cycling through London so much as swallowed by it, nothing to mark his progress except a never-ending sprawl of houses, the streets fanning out around him like concentric circles of hell.

He gets as far as Finsbury Park before he abandons the idea of cycling to the edge of town and takes the Tube instead, inadvertently getting on the Victoria Line rather than the Piccadilly. It takes less than ten minutes to reach the end of the line, and even with Ben's shaky grasp of geography it strikes him that this probably hasn't taken him much closer to where he wants to be.

Once he's through the ticket barriers, he hunts down a member of staff. 'Where are we?' he says. He notices the man glance at the large sign beside them. 'Look, I know we're in Walthamstow, but where are we in terms of, you know, *the bigger picture*?'

'Is this a religious thing?'

'I'm trying to get to Scotland.'

'You're on the London Underground. It doesn't go there.'

'You know what? Forget I mentioned Scotland. Let's say I want to go for a nice bike ride, heading north.'

And still the man just stares at him.

'Lee Valley's nice,' says a woman, standing nearby. 'That'll take you up in the direction of Hertford.'

'Which is still nowhere near Scotland,' says the man.

The woman points across a busy intersection. 'Just head in that direction until you get to the marshes. You can't miss it.'

*

The woman was right about the Lee Valley: it's such a stark green ribbon threading through North London, there was no way Ben could have missed it. Despite the industrial sprawl of the city pressing in on both sides, it feels to Ben as if London is loosening its grip with every turn of his pedals. It's a feeling that grows stronger and stronger as he wends northwards, until the path eventually slips under the M25 and Ben suddenly finds that he's broken free of the urban gravity and entered a completely different world; a place of open countryside and bucolic pleasures, the very concept of London now seeming remote.

If Alice was with him she would surely be greeting every tree, calling out to every bird and butterfly, perhaps even singing to the clouds overhead simply because they remind her of meringue. Ben wants to do the same, if only because she's not here to do it herself, but as he continues north it all begins to feel like too much effort. His pace has been sedate at best, but it's even slower now, his legs growing heavy beneath him. Even the bustle of colourful narrow boats moored at Roydon Marina isn't enough to excite him; he simply pedals past, wanting nothing but a cheap place to lie down and sleep. In that respect, Harlow has the rare opportunity of being something other than a disappointment. Never mind that Ben's hotel room has a view of a brick wall and some air-conditioning ducts, right now it's enough that it has a bed, a toilet and a lockable door. And as he drifts off to sleep, lying atop the duvet fully clothed, his only thought is of Alice and what she might have been doing today; how her bright and cheerful smile has doubtless brought joy to everyone she's met.

Mayfair, London W1

'You did *nothing*?' says Geneva. 'For two days?'

'Isn't that what sick people do?' replies Alice.

'No, not at all. On the rare occasion that I get sick, I spend the day fasting and visit this shamanic healer just off Harley Street. It works wonders.' She scribbles a name and website on one of her personal notelets, offers it to Alice. 'Here, for future reference…'

Alice takes it, certain that she couldn't even afford the card it's written on – embossed in gold, creamy to the touch – let alone the man himself. 'Thank you,' she says, wanting to be polite.

'You're welcome,' replies Geneva, smiling with a rare warmth; a humanity that Alice has never seen in her before. 'I'm just glad you're back.' Harry chooses this moment to start tugging at Alice's skirt. 'That's sweet, isn't it?' says Geneva. 'He's glad you're back too. Naturally, he doesn't feel the same about Glasgow.' She glances in the direction of Piers's office, his mere presence seeming to be an affront. 'I thought we were shot of him for a week at least.'

'Shouldn't we be glad he's on the mend?'

Geneva laughs. 'Really, Alice, the mad things you say. You can be quite amusing sometimes.' She holds out a file. 'Since you're so concerned, could you be a darling and take this to Glasgow for me?'

*

87

Alice finds Piers huddled at his desk, several shades paler than normal. He sits there bundled in thick layers, the look on his face suggestive of a boat in heavy seas.

'Alice,' he says, as she enters his office. 'A friendly face at last. That's exactly what I need right now.'

'Should you be here?' she replies.

'If I had to spend another day at home, I'd go mad. Anyway, I can tell that it's pissing everyone off that I've come back. The look of horror on their faces, it's priceless. I'm not poorly, you see, I'm an aesthetic disaster.'

'It is true that your skin tone is *very* last season.'

'I know. And vomiting blood is so passé.' He gestures for her to take a seat, the room feeling like their private lair. 'I hear you've been poorly too?'

'Don't worry about me,' she replies, not wanting to lie to him. 'I've already started planning the media pack.'

'Don't forget all the usual bullshit about it being great for kids, a good addition to a nutritious diet, blah, blah, blah.'

'Is any of that true?'

'Alice, truth is a very subjective term. Though that doesn't mean I don't believe in the product *wholeheartedly*.'

'What do you think about Suzie Franklin?' she says, unable even to say the name without getting excited. 'I don't know how Geneva did it.'

Piers looks away, shuffles through some papers. 'Let's not forget, that's the kind of thing that Geneva is paid to do. And she's good at it. I think she's the spawn of Satan, of course, but Lord knows she can whip together a guest list like no one else in London.'

'She's actually being quite nice this morning.' Alice sees the disbelief on his face. 'I know, it's... bizarre. But really, it's true.'

As though on cue, Geneva appears in the open doorway. 'You're both looking very cosy in here.'

'Alice and I were just discussing the media pack.'

'It is a tricky one,' replies Geneva, 'but I have no doubt that it's safe in Alice's hands.' She smiles the same sweet smile, and for an instant it feels like this is the beginning of a new bonhomie: that Geneva will be a pleasure to work with from now on, while Alice and Piers develop a special bond, becoming the Batman and Robin of London's PR industry. Then Geneva speaks again. 'Did you know that Alice has a secret boyfriend? A young man called Ben.'

Alice turns to Piers. 'I'd hardly call him my *boyfriend*.'

'But you are dating him,' says Geneva. 'You said so yourself.'

And still Alice tries to backpedal, speaking to Piers rather than Geneva. 'We're just, er, getting to know each other at the moment.'

'But Alice,' says Geneva, 'that's how it all starts. The next thing we know you'll have a baby on the way, and then you'll have a legitimate excuse to eat for two.'

Unsure what to say, Alice looks back at Piers, but finds that he's already busying himself with work. 'I'm very happy for both of you,' he says, all sense of camaraderie gone. 'I wish you every success together.'

*

As Alice heads for the safety of home that evening, it's food that fills her thoughts; the hypnotic rhythm of the train perfectly suited to a meditation on the dark arts of baking. How she could transform her sorrows into a red velvet cake, for instance, and then eat the whole thing, like some warrior tribesman cannibalizing the enemy.

Judging by her fellow passengers on the train, it's easy to believe that most of the people in London are returning home from a bruising day of frustrations and disappointments; that it's not just Alice who needs cake tonight, it's the whole world.

By the time she gets back to Feltham, there's nothing else she wants other than an evening of baking; knows that if she had the time and resources, she would happily make enough to share with the whole street – though perhaps not the violinist upstairs.

Unfortunately, Mei does not seem to share her belief in the redemptive power of food. 'That's what you're having for dinner?' she says. '*Cake?*'

'Why not?' replies Alice, sounding more defensive than she'd planned. Until seconds ago it had felt like a beautiful thing, surrendering all the cares of her day to an elaborate confection of cream and butter and sugar, but now, as she sees the horror on Mei's face, she can understand how it must look: a fat girl making enough cake for a church social. 'You're welcome to have some when it's ready.'

'And look like you? No way.' She stalks off, but then returns, her whole body as lithe and sinewy as a born predator. 'I'll be away this weekend.'

'Are you going anywhere nice?'

'None of your business. All you need to know is that if you go in my room while I'm gone, you're dead.'

Harlow, Essex

32 miles from Alice

It's late morning and Ben is returning from yet another visit to the hotel's vending machine when Dave calls. Struggling to hold three cans of Coke and five bags of crisps, Ben runs down the empty, silent corridor, fumbling with his key card as the ringing grows louder. Finally, he bursts into his room, tossing his haul of junk food onto the bed so he can answer the call. 'Dave, mate, how are you?'

'I'm good,' he replies, his tone more measured than usual. 'How's it going?'

Ben glances at his bike, neatly folded in the corner of the room. 'Yeah, things are all right. It's harder than I expected but, you know, you've just got to keep turning those pedals.'

'So where are you?'

'Er, I'm not even sure. It all looks the same after a while.'

'Because I'm guessing you're probably up around Peterborough.'

'Yeah, I think you're right. I think I saw a sign for that just now.'

'So you're taking a break at the moment?'

Ben kicks at an empty Coke can, adrift amid two days' worth of empty food wrappers. 'Yeah, that's right. Just a quick break.'

'And then you'll keep cycling, like you have been all morning?'

'Exactly.'

'You're a liar, Ben. I know where you are. I know you're in a hotel in Harlow. I know you've been there since Thursday.' Ben instinctively pulls back the curtains, peers into the car park. 'I'm not outside, Ben.' Spooked now, he steps back from the window, wonders if maybe the room is rigged with cameras. 'It's the bike, Ben. It's got a tracking chip in it. I can pinpoint your location within ten feet.'

'Where's the chip?'

'I'm not going to tell you that.'

'This feels like some Big Brother nightmare.'

'I didn't put it there to keep an eye on you. It's been there for ages, in case the bike gets stolen.'

'You could have at least told me.'

'I was going to, but then I thought it's for your safety too, or at least for my peace of mind. I need to know you're okay.'

'Thank you, Dr Evil. It sounds like you already knew everything, so there was no need to call, was there? You know that I've been in a hotel for two days doing nothing but watching bad TV and eating gummy bears.'

'But I don't know why,' he says, more gently now. 'Do you want to talk about it?'

'Cycling sucks, that's why. I feel like I've been in a plane crash. Everything hurts.'

'It'll get easier. Your body needs to adapt, that's all.'

'It's not just that, I haven't seen Alice for days and I'm—' He freezes, aware that he's just said too much.

'Mate, you haven't seen her for over a week.'

'That's what I mean. Over a week. And it's just getting to me, that's all.'

'But that's the whole point of the trip, isn't it? Going up there to try and find her?'

'Yeah, I suppose.' He sits on the bed and opens a can of Coke. 'It's funny. When I was in London, it felt like she was nearby somehow. And now, even though I should feel like I'm getting closer to her, it just feels like she's further and further away.'

'Then come home.'

'I don't want to go home. I want to go to Glasgow.'

'Then at least take the train up there.'

'But there's my granddad too. When he found out about the bike ride, I swear it was the only time I've ever seen him excited. My gran as well, for that matter. It was like the first time they've ever been proud of me.'

'Ben, I'm sure they'll love you no matter what you do.'

'But it's pretty obvious they'll love me even more on a bike.'

'Then sorry to state the obvious, but shouldn't you *be* on a bike?'

'I suppose you're right. I should get going…'

'Ben, I didn't call you to force you back on the road.'

'I saw a sign for Cambridge on the way here. Is that in the right direction?'

'Cambridge is in exactly the right direction. It's a nice place too. You'll like it.'

'I suppose it might even be educational, mightn't it? All those clever people. I might learn something.'

'Probably not by just cycling through it, but you never know.'

'If I leave now,' says Ben, with a sigh, 'I might get to Cambridge by this evening.'

'Can I offer you one piece of advice? If you're really going to ride all the way to Scotland, you may as well enjoy it. You're getting some exercise, you're seeing the countryside. What's not to love about that?'

*

It feels like being back in London at first, navigating busy streets while he tries to find the bike path heading north out of Harlow. It doesn't help that a chill wind is blowing, the dark clouds overhead suggesting that cold may soon be the least of his problems. In those first few minutes, he thinks of giving up, of going back to the hotel, perhaps even returning to London. Yet the longer he cycles, the less stiff his legs feel, and the easier it all becomes. By the time he's found a rhythm in his pedalling, he's leaving the town behind, heading north along quiet lanes into open countryside.

'Hello, Lower Sheering,' he shouts, as he rides through the first village. He hears a train in the distance, a reminder that there are quicker and easier ways to get from A to B, but still he persists, telling himself that this is the right thing to do. Just minutes after leaving the village he passes a sign marking the Hertfordshire county line and, in some small way, it feels like a victory; a reminder that he *is* making progress; that he's moving from one place to another. Buoyed by the thought, even his sedate pace begins to seem like a good thing; a chance to hear the birds singing, and to smell the damp earth of the freshly ploughed fields.

An hour later, he finds himself arriving in Bishop's Stortford with a weaker resolve. Being alone in the countryside was beautiful for a while, nothing to hear but the sound of the wind in the trees, but as soon as he spies the train station, he knows what he's going to do. Perhaps if he was stronger, fitter, and riding a proper bike rather than an evolutionary accident, he would power through this place; would zip across town and continue onwards through the countless villages beyond. Instead he allows the train to do it for him, taking care to find a window seat so that he can gaze out at the passing scenery: every village and distant manor house a milestone of sorts on his long journey north. And if Dave is still tracking him online, he will simply invent a new topography for this rolling landscape; will claim that it sloped so steeply down towards Cambridgeshire that he was able to freewheel at sixty or seventy miles an hour, moving across it like just another gust of wind.

He's been in Cambridge for less than twenty minutes when he decides to leave. He wanted to like it, wanted to fall in love with this fabled seat of learning, but it's the people who put him off. As he pushes his bike through town, all he sees is young men and women almost the same age as him, and yet in every other respect they are a different species, with their popped collars and self-confident swagger; so certain of their position in this world.

As he retraces his steps to the station, there's only one place that offers any prospect of consolation. Never mind that it's in completely the wrong direction; the past is calling and he can't stop now.

Feltham, West London

The day ends with such a magical sunset, even the rooftops of Feltham look pretty; the distant sound of aeroplanes taking off from Heathrow doing nothing to spoil the charm. With Mei away, Alice has spent the entire day swanning around the flat cooking and singing and listening to all her favourite music with total impunity. By the time Rachel arrives, Alice is so upbeat about her day that she's certain they really are on the brink of a new chapter in their lives: that soon they'll both be making progress in their careers and that these months of youthful confusion, of trying to find one's way in perennial debt-laden darkness, will at last be over.

'I can't believe you're actually cooking me dinner,' says Rachel.

'I would have done it sooner, but I can't entertain when Mei's here. It just seemed like such an opportunity with her gone.'

Rachel hands her a bottle of gin. 'This is all I could find at home. And there was no tonic, sorry.'

'Not to worry,' replies Alice, already worrying. 'I did get us a bottle of wine. Though it might not be very good. I sort of blew the budget on food, I'm afraid.'

'What are we having?'

'Beef wellington.' Even though she'll probably have to live on instant noodles until her next pay cheque, the words still make her smile. 'What's the point of having a job if I can't enjoy good food with a good friend?'

They pass Mei's bedroom, the door firmly closed. 'Are you not tempted to go in and have a look?' says Rachel.

'Knowing Mei, she's probably rigged the place like the Temple of Doom. Open the door even an inch and poisoned darts will come flying from all the walls.' She picks up the bottle of wine. 'Are you brave enough to try a glass?'

'Tell you what, why don't we save the wine for dinner? We could have a little shot of gin now. As a sort of aperitif.'

*

Alice can't decide if neat gin tastes progressively better or if it merely numbs one's senses, a sort of general anaesthetic. Certainly her fourth shot was an improvement on the third, and the fifth and sixth were better still. She floats around the kitchen in a fog now, her thoughts full of penguins, though she can't remember why.

In the living room, Rachel appears to be melting into the sofa, so that it seems conceivable she will soon disappear from view.

'How do you like your beef?' says Alice, trying not to slur her words.

'Dead.'

'That would be quite cruel, wouldn't it? Encasing a live animal in pastry.'

'I once had a cat that was very partial to puff pastry.'

'Though probably not being baked in it.' Standing there in the doorway, Alice's mind goes blank, no memory of what she was doing just moments ago. 'Have some more gin,' she says, stumbling towards Rachel and falling onto the sofa beside her. 'God, this is comfortable. Where did you get it?'

'Alice, this is your place.' She gazes around the room. 'Isn't it?'

'Oh, God, no, it's Mei's.' She pours them both another shot. 'I'd almost forgotten about her. I love life without her.'

'You don't need her,' slurs Rachel. 'You don't need anyone but me.'

'Do you think my parents would help me buy a place like this?'

'Your parents, maybe. My parents, definitely not.'

'Why would your parents want to help me buy a flat?'

'Exactly.'

Alice raises her glass. 'Let's drink to the future. To mine, to yours, to everybody's.'

'Everybody's except Mei's.'

'No,' says Alice, 'even to Mei's. Just nowhere near mine.'

★

Consciousness kicks in while Alice is eating beef wellington with her fingers. Across the table, Rachel's head is drooping closer and closer to her untouched food, a curtain of hair blocking her face from view.

'Rachel,' she says. 'Rachel.'

'No, no,' Rachel mumbles. 'If I have any more gin, I'll puke.'

'You need to eat.'

Rachel looks up, points a finger at Alice. 'No, *you* need to eat.'

'I am,' she says, her hands full of puff pastry.

'But not like before. It's not like the good old days.' Even drunk, Alice knows that this can only be a reference to the apex of Rachel's life: the three years they spent together as two socially awkward outsiders at Sheffield University; an under-achieving Goth, and a fat girl who was always trying too hard to please. 'You've changed,' says Rachel, her head drooping again, the tips of her hair now sitting in gravy. 'It used to be you and me against the world, and now it's just… now it's the world, isn't it? The big, awful world.' For a second, it appears that she's about to collapse onto her plate, but just as quickly she's raising her head and staring at the food, like she's forgotten what she's supposed to do with it. 'I think we should start on the wine.'

'That's probably not a very good idea,' says Alice.

'Tsk,' replies Rachel, already taking the bottle and twisting it open. She pours herself a hefty measure and takes a large mouthful. 'God, that's awful,' she says, nevertheless filling Alice's glass too. 'To best friends. Best friends forever.'

Alice takes a sip. 'Wow, that is bad.'

'It really, really is,' she says, the words sounding harder and harder to pronounce. She leans over the table and takes Alice's hand. 'But the only thing that matters is that we love each other. Like sisters separated at birth. Like… like twins.'

'Like non-identical twins.'

'Exactly. Non-identical twins. Born four and a half months apart. But, in every other respect, *twins*.' She downs her wine in one, appears more awake now. 'I have only two words for tomorrow: Netflix and pyjamas.'

'Oh, God, I can't,' says Alice, groaning. 'I've got to go to the homeless feeding tomorrow.'

'Just cancel.'

'I can't. I wasn't there last weekend either. Frida will have a fit if I don't go.'

'*Frida?* You should cancel just to punish her for having a name like that.' She shudders, hunches forward. 'Oh, God…'

'Are you okay?'

'I'm fine,' she says, refilling her wine glass. 'I'm just…' She grimaces, looking paler by the second. 'Correction. I'm going to throw up.'

Hand over her mouth, she jumps from her seat and runs for the nearest door.

'Not that one,' shouts Alice, as Rachel disappears into Mei's bedroom. Seconds later, she comes running back into the living room, her hand still clamped over her mouth, her eyes beginning to bulge. Before Alice has a chance to do anything, Rachel lurches to a stop in front of her and, much like Harry in the office, proceeds to bring up the contents of the last few hours, splashing them liberally across the carpeted floor.

Feltham, West London

When she first opens her eyes, Alice can't tell if the high-pitched screams of the violin are coming from her neighbour or her head. She lies stricken in bed, every cell of her body in anguish, Rachel gently snoring beside her. It doesn't help that the air is thick with the scent of detergent and air freshener – a chemical assault on the senses – Alice having been up most of the night, scrubbing the living room floor, trying to fix it before Mei gets home.

Leaving Rachel to sleep, Alice drags herself into the shower, and then out onto streets that seem too crowded and sunlit to be tolerable. Against all odds, she makes it across to Acton; arrives at the homeless feeding, as she aspires to every Sunday, to find Frida stirring a huge steaming vat of something or other, presiding over it as though preparing for a cult suicide.

'I know they don't like chilli con carne,' says Frida, in lieu of a greeting, 'but I can only serve what I'm given. What else am I supposed to do with a load of minced beef and enough kidney beans to sink a ship?'

'They don't *all* hate it,' replies Alice. Thinking that this may lack her hallmark optimism, she tries again. 'Some of them love it.'

'But they're not the ones who say anything, are they? It's only ever the moaners who get vocal.' Frida keeps stirring the pot, the clouds of steam giving her hair a frazzled appearance, the perfect complement to her personality. 'But even the moaners, they're not the ones I blame. It's the government.' This is a subject that Frida inevitably mentions whenever they meet, but today is the first time that she's started talking politics before Alice has even taken off her coat. 'I'd love to feed this entire pot to the Prime Minister and her cronies. And not by mouth, I can tell you that much.'

'If you're wondering why I'm still wearing sunglasses,' says Alice, 'I have, er, a bit of a migraine today. I'm going to keep them on for a while, if you don't mind.'

'Why would I care about a pair of sunglasses when society itself is disintegrating all around us? If you need any better example of how bad things have got, take a look at me. I've been a strict vegan for twenty years. I don't even wear leather. And what am I doing? Stirring a bloody great pot of dead cow, and all because there are people starving on our streets.' She stops stirring. 'You're still a meat eater, aren't you?' She says it with a hint of disgust. 'Could you try this for me?'

'Of course,' replies Alice.

Frida watches as she takes a small spoonful, the molten mixture requiring lots of blowing to cool it down. 'That beef would have been factory farmed,' she says, as Alice eventually puts it in her mouth. 'The animals would have had brutal, diseased lives, and died in agony.'

Alice forces herself to swallow. 'It's quite spicy,' she says, unsure whether she should compliment a militant vegan on her beef chilli. 'But I'm sure they'll love it. Even the moaners.'

*

As it happens, the giant vat of chilli provokes neither moaning nor love. Everyone simply takes what they're given, too grateful for a meal to care about the balance of spices or the ethics of animal husbandry. Alice takes off her sunglasses for the feeding, determined to look everyone in the eye as she plates up food and hands out bread rolls, though on several occasions she notices people do a double-take, doubtless

106

wondering what kind of night could have left her looking like that. As she serves these people – the elderly, always as quiet as church mice; the young families, their wide-eyed children transfixed by the prospect of food, perhaps the first of the day – she wishes she could tell them that it's not mere sustenance, but rather that it represents her heartfelt best wishes too: that their circumstances may soon take a turn for the better; that they may soon have a home of their own, with cupboards full of food. The hangover still pounds behind her eyes, her limbs still ache from a night spent scrubbing the floor, but right now, in this instant, none of it matters because every time she smiles at these people she knows that she's doing something good.

'So, how are things?' says Frida, as they clean up later that afternoon.

'Fine,' replies Alice, unaccustomed to her being friendly. 'Busy at work. The usual.'

'And your love life?'

She briefly considers mentioning Ben. 'Nothing to report.'

'If you're free next Saturday, I'm having a party at my place. There's a guy I'd like you to meet.' Even though it seems utterly implausible that someone like Frida could ever introduce her to a man she'd want to date, Alice feels herself blush. 'His brother's being released from prison in the next few days. We're having a party in his honour.' She evidently sees the blush drain from Alice's face. 'Don't worry, he's not a criminal, he's an *eco-warrior*. He got six months for sabotaging a fracking well.'

'Ah, I see,' says Alice, eager to stall for time, her mind already racing ahead to the prospect of family get-togethers with this potential suitor: everyone sitting down to a vegan casserole, while the brother regales them with tales of prison rape.

'Look,' says Frida, 'you don't have to give me an answer right now. Just think it over and let me know.'

★

By the time that Alice gets home, shortly before four o'clock, her hangover has taken on existential proportions: pounding proof that everything in her life is wrong. She finds Mei on the sofa, sitting silently in the chemical fog of the flat.

'You cleaned,' is all she says, as Alice enters the room.

'We're flatmates,' replies Alice.

'No, you're my lodger.'

'I prefer "flatmate".'

'But then no one would know that the whole flat is mine. That I own it, not you.'

'Well, strictly speaking, your parents own it.'

'Only until they die. Then it's mine.' She says it so matter-of-factly, Alice can only assume that she spends a lot of time anticipating her parents' deaths. 'You don't need to clean the carpet.'

'Are you not happy?' says Alice.

'No, I like it. It smells—' *Deadly*, thinks Alice. *Carcinogenic*. 'Very clean.'

'At first I wasn't going to do it, but then I thought, I have some spare time, so why not? Spring cleaning, that kind of thing.'

Mei appears satisfied – is perhaps even secretly thrilled that Alice has prostrated herself in this manner. 'But don't do it again,' she says. 'You'll probably be a lodger all your life. You shouldn't waste your energy.' She looks at the floor, so clean it appears luminescent. 'And anyway, if I thought the carpets were dirty, I would just tell my father to buy me new ones.'

Alice thinks of her own father, presumably home from his model train exhibition by now. 'Don't worry,' she tells Mei, already retreating to her bedroom, 'you have my word that I will never clean the carpet again.'

'There's a strange girl in there,' says Mei. Alice pauses, her hand already on the door handle. 'She's been farting in her sleep.'

'Don't worry, she'll be leaving soon.'

As she steps into her room, it becomes obvious that this is unlikely. Rachel lies there, fast asleep, looking and sounding much like a beached sea mammal. Taking a seat by the window, Alice calls her father, certain that his calm and steady voice will make everything about the day, and the world, seem better. She smiles to herself in anticipation, but doesn't even get the satisfaction of hearing a ring at the other end of the line; instead, she's shunted straight through to voicemail, while Rachel begins to snore in the background.

Great Yarmouth, Norfolk
122 miles from Alice

The sun is already beginning to set when Dave finally joins Ben. He says nothing as he sits down beside him, the two of them on a bench looking out at the dark expanse of the North Sea.

At length, Ben speaks. 'I thought you might come. That GPS thing is pretty good, isn't it?'

'Have you really been sitting here all day?'

'Pretty much,' says Ben, still staring out to sea. 'Most of yesterday evening too.'

'Do you want to tell me why we're in Great Yarmouth?' He waits, but Ben doesn't reply. 'It's a bit of a detour, isn't it? For the man who was supposed to be heading north. I presume you didn't think much of Cambridge.'

'It was full of wankers in stuck-up collars, and blokes trying to paddle boats with long sticks. It's mad; all these rich kids and no one can afford a couple of oars.' He takes a deep breath, sighs. 'I thought coming here might help, but to be honest I only feel more depressed.'

'How could coming to Great Yarmouth help with

anything? It's the tattooed-head capital of the world; the kind of place where a six-pack of lager is considered a balanced breakfast.'

'We used to come here every summer when I was a kid, me and my grandparents.' He gazes across the empty beach, the whole place looking cold and unloved in the fading light. 'They were happy-sad holidays, you know what I mean? I got to play on the beach and we all ate ice cream, but I don't know…' For a moment, they sit in silence again, nothing to hear but the sound of waves crashing on the shore. 'All the other kids were with their mums and dads, like a proper family holiday. I know the place is a bit of a shithole, but some things don't matter, do they? Not when you have each other.'

'Those years must have been hard, Ben, but if your parents could see you now, they'd be so proud.'

'I'm not so sure about that.'

'You're a good bloke.'

'You think?' he says, distractedly. 'Maybe I've just got good pills…' Before Dave can reply, he speaks again. 'Have I ever told you why I like listening to the sea? I like thinking how it sounds the same even after we're long dead.'

'Mate, that's a bit morbid.'

'No, it's not, it's comforting. If you close your eyes and just listen. It's nice to know that the sea sounded exactly like that to ancient Romans and Vikings and, I don't know, Emily Brontë. To my mum and dad too.' He listens to the waves for a few more moments, smiling to himself. 'Just for the record,' he says, turning to face Dave, 'I *am* still cycling to Scotland. I'm just taking the scenic route.'

'Ben, by no stretch of the imagination is this the scenic route to Scotland. Not to mention that there hasn't been much cycling so far.'

'That's not fair. I was cycling yesterday. For a while, anyway.'

'I thought this might help you focus.' Dave hands him a

piece of folded paper, watches as he opens it, a picture of smiling children coming into view. 'Since you didn't have time to find a charity before you set off, I found one for you. It's for kids who've lost their parents.'

'I thought you wanted me to stop the ride?'

'I do, but I also know how bloody-minded you are. No matter what I say, I know you'll persist at it, drifting off who knows where. At least this way, you'll have a real purpose, and be doing some genuine good in the process.'

Ben stares at the children's smiles. 'Yeah, it's a nice idea. And it's not like I've done anything else with my life, is it?'

'Mate, that's not why I'm suggesting it. Agnes was thinking we could put something on the market stall. Encourage more people to sponsor you.'

'Though we're going to have to fib a bit. I've spent most of my time on trains.'

'Then we'll just go back to wherever you stopped cycling yesterday and start from there.'

'Piss off, I'm not going back anywhere. And there's no point starting from here, we're miles off course.' From Dave's expression, it's obvious he doesn't approve. 'Look at it this way,' says Ben. 'The sooner I get to Glasgow, the sooner all those little orphans will get their money.'

Somewhere near Battersea, London SW11

It's only as the crowded train grinds to a halt for the third time that the conductor makes an announcement about signal failures; a carefully worded apology that avoids any mention of how long they might be stuck there between stations, unable to do anything but sigh.

Like so many others in the carriage, Alice finds herself checking her watch yet again. The good news is that it's only one minute later than when she last looked; the bad news is that she's now almost forty minutes late. Even if the train started moving this instant, not only racing headlong into Waterloo, but in fact leaving the tracks altogether and flying over the rooftops of Central London, she would only just get to work in time for the weekly team meeting. In itself, this doesn't seem like such a bad thing – the meeting often ends up feeling like a live-fire exercise – but today more than usual it seems to Alice that she *needs* to be there. The look on Piers's face on Friday remains fresh in her mind: how he reacted to the news of Ben; how a careless fiction seemed to deal a blow to their nascent alliance.

Further down the carriage, she notices a man she's seen a few times in the last week or two. He sits there, so absorbed in his newspaper, she allows herself more than the usual amount of time to take in the details: his neatly clipped beard, his beautiful shirt, his air of total self-assurance.

He looks up.

Their eyes meet.

She looks away.

Definitely married, she thinks to herself. It would have been his wife who picked the shirt, naturally. While also styling their house for a *Vogue* photo shoot. And juggling the demands of a global business empire.

Feeling herself spiral downwards on a wave of comparisons, she commands herself to stop; to be positive. Everything in her life will get better, if only she keeps believing! At that precise moment the train starts to crawl forward, and even the mood in the carriage begins to lift. *I did this*, she thinks to herself. *This is the power of positivity!* Her mind is beginning to race with all the possibilities for self-transformation – how she will build the future of her dreams one positive day at a time – when the train lurches to a stop yet again, signal failure suddenly seeming emblematic of life itself.

*

The team meeting has finished when Alice finally reaches the office, everyone spilling from the conference room with the look of people who've just survived a long siege.

Geneva approaches her, Harry tucked under one arm.

'Sorry for being late,' says Alice. 'I do have an excuse.'

'Please,' she replies, 'I think missing that meeting was the only clever thing you've done in months.' She thrusts Harry into Alice's arms. 'He's boring me. Would you take him for a while?'

'You want me to take him out? I've only just arrived.'

'Jesus, Alice, you can be very literal. I don't care *where* you take him. Just take him. You could take him to the pantry, for instance, and show him how many calories you're capable of adding to a single cup of coffee. Even a dog should find that entertaining.'

Alice is still standing there, confused, when Piers approaches. 'Why are you holding that thing?'

'To be honest,' she replies, 'I'm not sure if I'm allowed to put him on the floor.'

'And there's no point asking the bitch from hell, is there? She's breathing more than the usual fire today.'

'Did the meeting not go well? I'm sorry I missed it.'

'Don't be. I spent most of it wanting to lock them all in there and set fire to the place.'

'Well, I'm here now. You're not alone.'

He smiles. 'I was thinking we might have lunch tomorrow, if you're up for it.'

'Yes!' replies Alice, so relieved that she doesn't even think of curbing her enthusiasm. 'I'd love to.'

'Perfect. I'll find somewhere suitably lavish. My treat, of course.'

Ely Cathedral, Cambridgeshire
64 miles from Alice

'When you said you wanted to show me something,' says Ben, breathless, 'this isn't quite what I had in mind.' He follows Dave up a steep, winding staircase, climbing higher and higher. 'I should be saving my energy for the ride.'

'Think of the view when we get to the top,' replies Dave, gasping the words. 'And think of the history. This place was built in the thirteenth century. Imagine all the people who've climbed up these stairs in the last eight hundred years.'

'All of whom are now dead, I would like to point out. And for all we know, this was what finished them off.'

They climb in silence after that, neither of them seeming capable of words. It's only as they reach the top of the West Tower, bursting into the cold morning air, that Ben speaks. 'Bloody hell.'

'I don't think you can say that kind of thing in a church.'

'But the view…' He goes to the parapet wall and leans against it. 'It's like being on a ship up here. We could have a little *Titanic* moment, the two of us. I don't even mind being the Kate to your Leonardo, as long as you keep your cock to yourself.'

'That's where you'll be heading,' says Dave, pointing out to the northwest. 'Towards Peterborough.'

'No, I've decided to go due north. I reckon it stays flatter for longer that way.'

'But you should be going in that direction.'

'Then I'll just turn left later.'

'Hills are inevitable at some point, Ben, given that you're heading for the Peak District.'

'And I'm going to pretend that I didn't hear you say that.'

'Well, whichever way you go, it's all the Fens. Flat as a pancake, the lot of it. Though it is very, *very* flat. It might get a bit boring after a while.'

Ben snorts. 'Not likely, mate. Flat is my favourite word. I don't mind if it stays flat like this forever.'

*

Even by mid-afternoon, Ben still feels the same way; still feels that this ride is exactly what he should be doing. Yes, his legs ache from all the exercise, but the sun is shining and the path ahead of him stretches far into the distance, as straight and flat as an arrow, the landscape so empty and featureless that it's hard to even gauge his speed or progress.

He's cycling alongside a wide channel of water when his grandmother calls.

'Gran,' he says, pulling to a stop.

'Benjamin, darling, how did you know it was me?'

'Because I can see it on my phone.'

'Like a premonition, you mean? Maybe you have the gift.'

'No, it's—'

'Can you see how many fingers I'm holding up?'

'Is everything okay, Gran?'

She sounds confused now. 'Of course it is. Why are you calling?'

'You called me.'

'Oh, yes, it's Neville. He's very ill. He's stopped eating and he looks depressed.'

Given that he's going to be stuck in a cage for the next sixty years, Ben marvels that this hasn't happened sooner. 'What does the vet say?'

'He can't see him until tomorrow. All he said is we should keep him in a dark, warm place for a while, and see how he gets on.'

'Like a loaf of bread,' replies Ben. 'After an hour or two, you'll probably find he's risen to twice the size.'

At the other end of the line, Ben can hear the muffled voice of his grandfather, doubtless sitting in his usual armchair, absorbed in the same old book.

'Your grandfather wants to know if you're in the Peak District yet.'

Ben glances at his surroundings: a landscape so relentlessly horizontal, it's impossible to imagine that hills exist on the same planet. 'Not exactly.'

She shouts the reply to her husband. 'He says not yet.' In response, there's more baritone mumbling. 'Benjamin, your grandfather wants to know when you expect to get there.'

'Look, I'll let you know, okay?'

'He'll let you know,' she shouts to her husband. She starts speaking to Ben again, the words still so loud they're clearly intended for a wider audience. 'If only he'd take the same interest in Neville as he does the Peak District.'

'Gran, if the vet's told you to just put Neville in a cupboard for a while, I'm sure everything will be fine.' *Or not*, he thinks, *which would also be fine.*

'Will you pray for him?'

119

The question catches Ben off guard. In all the years he's known her, she's never mentioned God. Even in his childhood, she never referenced the role that a god may play in the broken-glass landscape of his new life, never indulged him with baby-talk of his parents being needed as angels. And yet here she is, trying to enlist divine intervention for a parrot.

Before Ben can reply, his grandmother is speaking again. 'Oh, I can hear Neville calling me. I need to go.'

Mayfair, London W1

After being absent from the office for most of the morning, Piers meets Alice at the restaurant, a place of handsome waiters and heavy, leather-bound wine lists.

'When you said lavish,' says Alice, sliding into their banquette, 'I didn't expect *this* lavish.'

'Tuesdays always feel like champagne days to me.' He gives her a disarming smile. 'We'll finish with a big fat espresso and I promise you'll glide through the afternoon on a wave of fresh inspiration.'

'This isn't the Piers I'm used to,' she says, blushing at the rash indulgence of it all.

He gives her another smile, even warmer than the first. 'Then it's about time we changed that.'

*

Champagne on an empty stomach leaves Alice feeling as though her whole body is effervescing, her entire bloodstream fizzing with tiny bubbles of wonderfulness.

'I'll probably regret this later on,' she says, as she accepts another glass.

'You're too young for regrets,' says Piers, a playful look in his eyes. While she blushes again, he fixes her with a more probing look. 'Isn't it mad that we work together every day and yet I know almost nothing about your personal life?'

'I seem to spend most of it in the kitchen these days. I'm becoming a bit of a baker.'

'How lovely.'

'It is, actually. There's something very primal and nurturing about baking a cake. I know everyone else in the office aspires to be a size-zero supermodel, but I just want a house that always smells of freshly baked cookies and scones. I mean, when I'm not busy with my career, of course.'

'Please, we're having lunch as friends. It's all off the record.'

'Besides baking, there's really nothing else to tell, other than a mad flatmate, and a mad friend, and… well, you probably spot the theme.'

'Relationships can be difficult.' He leans closer. 'You learn a thing or two about them when you've been married for twenty years.'

'Twenty years already?'

'We were still at uni when we met. A fine, fine woman, but I wouldn't say it was the best decision I ever made.'

'It is very young to get married.'

'The trouble is you feel invincible at that age. You think every idea you have is the best ever.'

'Been there, done that, I'm afraid. I got my tongue pierced when I was nineteen.' She sees the surprise on his face. 'It seemed like a good idea at the time. It was only when I had a bloody great hole in my mouth that I came to my senses. Though if nothing else, it taught me that life can go back to normal quite quickly if you make the right decisions.'

'If only everything was so easy to fix.'

In the wistful silence that follows, Alice can think only of cementing their bond, of sharing a confidence. 'I'm not dating Ben. Geneva misunderstood a…' She hesitates over the right words. 'A complex situation. Ben is just someone I met very briefly, in the park.'

'Two gentle souls who touched one another in some way, and then parted for evermore.'

'Something like that, yes.'

'But perhaps it's just as well that I thought you were dating Ben. It was a rallying call of sorts.' For a few seconds it looks like he's reaching across the table, but then he's fiddling with his champagne flute, his hand gradually working its way backwards in a slow rearrangement of cutlery, side plate and napkin.

Watching him, Alice feels a vague sense of alarm, but then she's rolling forward on another wave of champagne, the alcohol carrying yet more words from her mouth. 'Can you believe it, someone I know is trying to set me up with a *vegan*?'

'No!'

'Exactly. I'm still not sure how I'd tell him that the entire bottom layer of my food pyramid is made of bacon.'

'You should learn from my mistakes, Alice. Don't end up with the wrong person.' Another silence now. 'And remember that an opportunity for pleasure is sometimes right there in front of you, day after day. You just need to see it.'

As his hand begins another slow advance across the table, Alice wishes that she hadn't started drinking, hadn't agreed to come. 'I'm afraid my head's a little too fuzzy,' she says. 'I think I won't be able to stay for lunch after all.'

Piers looks alarmed. 'You haven't eaten anything yet.'

'I can grab a sandwich on the way back to the office.'

'Don't leave because you're frightened, Alice. I'm frightened too, but I'm still here.'

'I think it's best,' she says, already sliding off the banquette, 'that we just pretend none of this happened.'

Piers's hand darts forward, wraps itself around hers. 'Alice, I've already got us a hotel room. We can go there now.'

The Fens, near Wisbech, Cambridgeshire
84 miles from Alice

Ben's been cycling all morning, and yet still he's excited by the prospect of a full day: nothing but birdsong and the gentle purr of the spinning wheels. At this moment, it feels like the landscape was made for him: nothing about it to challenge his novice cycling skills, nothing to tax his embarrassing bike. Instead just the steady turning of the pedals, a hypnotic cadence, the tempo unchanged for hours on end.

There's no news of Neville, which Ben assumes is good, though frankly Neville could have dropped dead and it still wouldn't qualify as *bad* news.

'I wouldn't mind some company right now,' he says, hopeful that the words may conjure Alice. 'I think you'll be very impressed with my cycling skills. I reckon I'm almost as good as you are now.' He looks down at his bike. 'Though I do look a total plonker on this thing.' He glances around, even behind, still hopeful of spotting Alice, but there's no sign of her; no sign of anything, in fact, just this eternal landscape stretching out in all directions, an endless patch-work of fields and waterways. 'Looking on the bright side, I suppose not seeing you is a good sign. I'm obviously not losing my mind; I'm not a *total* nut job. Maybe I'm even cured, who knows? Maybe I don't need my medication anym—' He slams on the brakes. 'Bloody hell, I forgot to take my pills.'

Jumping off the bike and letting it fall to the ground, he rummages through his bag, digs out the pill box that has been his constant companion for the last eight years. He slides back the lid and stares down at the contents: red, green and blue pills; colourful little substitutes for all the things he will never be.

Not for the first time, he hesitates, wonders what would happen if he simply put them back in his bag; if he conven-iently forgot to take them. Would it be days or even just hours before he noticed a change? Would he even be aware of it, the slow tipping of his existence back into the chaos of his teenage years?

'It could well be,' he says, as he empties the pills into his hand, 'that you're the only good things about me. That everything half-decent about my personality is made in a factory somewhere. The rest is just...' *Erratic. Unpredictable. Prone to strange, inappropriate statements.* 'Let's just say, less than perfect.'

He starts swallowing them, grateful that Alice isn't there to see it; isn't there to witness his dependency on these pills, each one a reminder that he's not like everyone else. As he takes the last of them, he tries to picture what's happening to him inside: the pills dissolving into a rainbow-hued cloud of optimism and self-control, filling every inch of him so thoroughly that, for another twenty-four hours, he is complete again; impossible anymore to see where he ends and the pills begin.

Grosvenor Square Garden, London W1

'I can't believe people drink to calm their nerves,' says Alice, calling Rachel from a bench in the park. 'All that champagne is just making everything seem ten times worse.'

'You're the only person I know who complains about free champagne.'

'And unwanted advances. From the man who employs me. The *married* man who employs me.' She takes a mouthful of coffee, desperate to sober up. 'What am I supposed to say when we see each other in the office?'

'I suggest you just march in there, slap his face, and threaten to blackmail him.'

'That's probably against the law.'

'Then just slap him and resign.'

'God, no. I need the job.'

'You can find another.'

'Yes, in some parallel universe where twenty-two-year-olds are in popular demand. I spend my Sundays feeding the homeless, I don't want to *be* one of them too.'

'Okay, I've got an idea. How about *I* threaten to blackmail him and we split the money?'

'I find it a little disturbing that you're about to start a management programme.'

'I never claimed I was going to be good at it.'

Alice notices Geneva crossing the square, presumably heading back to the office. 'I've just spotted my boss.'

'The one who wants to have sex with you?'

'No, the evil one. The one with the dog.' Geneva sees her, appears to do a double-take before heading in her direction. 'Oh, God, she's coming over. I've got to go.'

She hangs up before Rachel can even say goodbye; tries to look relaxed.

'I thought you were having lunch with Piers?' says Geneva, clearly on the scent of gossip.

'I was, but, er, the champagne went to my head, so I had to cut it short.' She holds up her cup of coffee, as if it's something medicinal; prescribed proof of a physical disorder. 'To be honest, I don't approve of drinking alcohol at lunchtime. It seems wrong to be drunk in the office.'

'Give it a few more years and you'll much prefer it that way.' Geneva turns to leave. 'Will you walk with me?' Alice knows her well enough to understand that this is not a suggestion. Reluctantly, she gets up, the two of them walking side by side. 'I presume Piers took you somewhere very expensive?'

'It certainly looked like it,' replies Alice.

'He believes himself to have impeccable taste. Only the best will do for Piers.' She glances at Alice again, a smirk on her face. 'But look on the bright side. By ducking out of lunch, you've avoided who knows how many calories. You can think of it as the first step on the long journey ahead of you.'

The Fens, South Lincolnshire
98 miles from Alice

The day's ride ends at a small bed and breakfast, the garden neatly trimmed, the windows prim with lace curtains.

Even though he has no booking, the landlady greets him with a familiarity better suited to family members. 'I'm Janet, welcome to my home,' she says, already reaching for him with open arms. 'No one comes into this house without a hug.'

She pulls him into a tight embrace, pressing herself against him for a little too long. Standing there, swaddled, Ben wonders whether the plumber gets the same treatment; can imagine frightened Mormons preferring to shout their message of salvation from the garden gate.

She shows him to a shed at the back of the house, watching a little too attentively as he puts the bike away. After locking the door, she makes a show of putting the key in her breast pocket. 'Anytime you want it, day or night,' she says, patting her bosom, 'you know where to come.'

'Thanks,' replies Ben, already wondering how quickly he can get to his room and wedge the door shut.

He follows her indoors, every room a reminder of why no one misses the seventies.

'This is yours,' she says, as she opens a door to reveal a space swaddled in nothing but pink.

'Christ,' says Ben, 'it's madder than I am.' In the awkward seconds that follow, he suspects that he may have spoken without thinking. 'What I mean is, it's lovely. Thank you.'

Janet goes to the bedside, starts fluffing his pillows. 'You must be famished. Would you like me to make you some dinner?'

Even if he didn't have a bag full of chocolate bars, he'd still say no. 'I'm okay, thanks. I plan on getting an early night.'

'Then maybe a glass of hot milk to help you sleep?'

'To tell you the truth, I'm so knackered, I'll probably nod off in no time.'

'Of course, of course, I understand.' She puts his pillow down, taking care to smooth the bedspread as she goes. 'But if there's anything I can do for you, anything at all, you just let me know. My bedroom is right across the hall.'

The Fens, South Lincolnshire

98 miles from Alice

Ben wakes to early-morning sunlight coming through thin pink curtains, the whole room glowing with a rosy lumines-cence. Despite expecting Janet to burst in at any moment, the night was uneventful, only the occasional squeak of a floorboard reminding him that he wasn't alone in the house.

Muscles aching, he goes down for breakfast, finds the dining table set for one. He's still standing there, looking at it, when Janet enters the room. 'Good morning! Did you sleep well?'

'Like a log.'

She smiles – perhaps already aware of this, who's to know? 'I'm going to make you a big breakfast to see you on your way. Are you going far?'

'Scotland.' And suddenly it doesn't matter that Ben finds her a little mad and creepy, he would stay there all over again just to see the look on her face: the sheer wonder, as though he'd just said he was cycling to Timbuktu.

'That's amazing,' she says. 'Such an adventure.'

'I'm doing it for charity,' he adds, wanting to milk this moment for all it's worth; this rare sensation of doing something special.

'My Malcolm works in Scotland.' She sinks onto one of the chairs, the mere mention of his name seeming to drain her of the energy to remain standing. 'I'd like him to work closer to home, of course, but the money's good up there. Out in the oilfields.'

Unsure whether Malcolm is a son or a husband, Ben just nods sympathetically. 'It must be hard for you.'

'Well, it is, but at least I don't have to worry about him being with other women, do I? Stuck on an oil rig in the middle of the North Sea.' The thought appears to comfort her, but just as quickly her face clouds with new fears. 'Though of course the whole thing could blow up at any second. It's just a big floating bomb, when you think about it.' As her eyes fill with tears, she glances around the room, maybe cataloguing all the possessions that have been bought with sleepless nights and constant worry. 'It's funny, isn't it? My biggest fear is that something will happen to him and I'll be left on my own, but the truth is I've been on my own for years.' She stands up, blinks away the tears. 'Anyway, ignore me—'

'But if you need to talk about it.'

'No, no, I'm fine.' She smooths down her apron and forces a big smile. 'Now, you stay exactly where you are. There's one breakfast coming right up.'

*

When Janet finally brings his breakfast, it looks more like a greeting card than something to eat. Around the edge of the plate, she's used tomato ketchup to pipe the words 'Ben's breakfast'. In the middle are heart-shaped fried eggs, a bacon smile and two shiny tomato eyes: an edible celebration of all the love and companionship that doesn't exist in her life.

She offers no commentary as she puts it in front of him, simply smiles and then retreats from the room, perhaps feeling that she's already said too much.

He doesn't see her again until he's almost ready to leave. 'I hate to think of you getting hungry out there,' she says, handing him some sandwiches, neatly wrapped. 'I don't get the chance to talk about Malcolm very often. Thank you.' She pulls him into another embrace. 'Ride safely!'

'I will,' he replies, fighting the urge to wriggle free; certain that Janet needs to do this for her own sake rather than his.

It's as he's getting on his bike that he wonders what Alice would say at this moment; how she'd make the day glow, a ray of golden sunshine.

'Good luck with the business,' he says. 'I've had a… a lovely stay.' He watches her face light up at these harmless untruths. 'You've been a wonderful host.' Her smile grows radiant now, and to look at her he can imagine that she will keep smiling long after he's gone.

The 08:05 to London Waterloo

This is not a day for lists, not unless they involve miraculously finding another job or plotting an early demise for Piers. This is certainly not a day for trying to find silver linings in life's dark clouds. Even Alice's fellow passengers appear ill-tempered and sour today, not helped by the total absence of Mr Mystery; doubtless at home having passionate, deeply fulfilling sex with his supermodel wife. For the third time this morning.

Looking at the fat drops of rain running down the windows, it's easy to imagine that the sun will never shine again; that Alice's whole life will pass beneath this same grey sky, her hair turning white and her teeth falling out while she keeps going back to work day after day.

She carries this heavy heart all the way into Waterloo, through the masses of people on the ticket concourse, and down into the Underground, the long walk to the Jubilee Line a daily reminder that she's not there yet, in every sense.

When she eventually gets to the office, it's some comfort that Piers is still absent, no sign that he's been there since she left him in the restaurant yesterday. It's tempting to imagine that he went to their hotel room and accidentally choked to death on a bag of nuts, but then she abandons the thought, not because it's unkind to imagine him dead, but rather because it will only heighten the disappointment when she inevitably finds that he's not.

She's just started Googling new hamster memes when Piers bursts upon her, taking a seat on the edge of her desk. 'Alice, I think we should talk about what happened yesterday.'

'Absolutely,' she replies, trying to calm her nerves. 'In fact, I've been looking forward to seeing you again, so we can, you know, *discuss it.*'

'Look, the bottom line is we'd both had a bit too much to drink.' Alice feels burning words of protest in her mouth, but nothing comes out. 'My attitude is that we should both just forget all about it and leave it in the past.'

'Okay,' she croaks.

'I knew you'd feel the same way as me.' The words provoke a fond smile, perhaps thinking of all the other things they could have felt together. 'The point is what's done is done. We've got work to do, mountains to climb.' He reaches over and gives her shoulder a chummy squeeze. 'It's onwards and upwards, Alice. Onwards and upwards.'

The Fens, south Lincolnshire
103 miles from Alice

The weather could just as easily apply to Ben's mood: in the last couple of hours a storm front has rolled in, bringing with it dark skies and the prospect of heavy rain. And though logically it will pass sooner or later, right now it looks and feels as if the world is coming to an end; that the gentle landscape of yesterday is actually just a featureless, never-ending theatre of death.

Taking refuge in an open-sided picnic pagoda, he calls Dave on his mobile while the wind begins to gust and the rain starts to fall. 'I want to know the weather forecast,' he says, as soon as Dave answers.

'That sort of depends on where you are right now.'

'You're the creepy stalker with the GPS thing.'

'Okay, hold on,' says Dave, leaving Ben in silence, nothing to fill his thoughts but the sound of the wind and the rain. 'All right, I found you. You're in south Lincolnshire. To be honest that's not great progress in two days of cycling.'

'Piss off, Dave. I just want to know what the weather's going to be doing for the rest of the day.'

Another long silence. 'Hmm,' says Dave. 'Let's just say this: you're probably going to get wet.'

'Well, I'm glad we've established that,' replies Ben, barely able to shelter from the rain now, the wind blowing it sideways. 'How did people cope before technology?'

'And the outlook for the rest of the day is, well, it doesn't matter.'

'No, tell me.'

'It's pretty bad.'

Ben's known Dave long enough to understand that a comment like that does not bode well: Dave could see a twenty-storey tidal wave approaching and say it looks 'pretty bad'; could see the Grim Reaper culling people at the super-market and say it looks 'pretty bad'.

'So, in other words, I'm screwed?'

'Just keep going. Think of the orphans.'

'Yeah, all warm and dry, the little fuckers. How many sponsors do I have?'

A moment of hesitation. 'Well, you know, we're getting there.'

'Please tell me I have more than you and Agnes.'

'Look,' replies Dave, clearly struggling to put a positive spin on things, 'you just need to give it some time.'

Unlike so many things in life, time does not improve the situation. When Ben sets off again, the wind is blowing so hard he has nothing to lose by leaving the picnic shelter; he's already soaked to the skin. Out in the full force of the storm, the rain quickly works its way into his eyes, his ears, his mouth. He tries to remember the near-hypnotic rhythm of his pedalling yesterday, when this place seemed like the very best of England. 'If I can just get back into a rhythm,' he shouts over the sound of the rain, but the wind and his cold, wet clothes make every turn of the pedals feel Herculean. 'And only a few more hundred miles to go,' he shouts. 'This really was the best decision of my life.'

He pictures telling Alice about this moment; how valiant it will seem that he rode through hell and high water simply to be by her side – and yet even that's not enough right now.

'Let's face it,' he says to himself, 'she could have anyone.' As soon as the words are out, his imagination starts to run with them: how she probably spends her nights in the arms of someone better than him; someone who doesn't need pills to be a functional adult; someone richer, stronger, and faster on a bicycle.

The rain drips from his face like tears, and although he tries to hunker down and keep pedalling, without the hope of being with Alice, there's nothing left in him. As the pedalling becomes harder, Ben imagines that it's symptomatic of a broken heart: that love is what sends us freewheeling through life, and, in its absence, we are each left struggling in the pouring rain. It's only as the bike grows increasingly sluggish beneath him that he notices his rear tyre: the way it's beginning to surrender to his bodyweight, growing flatter and flatter just like his dreams.

'Are you kidding me?' he shouts, screaming the words into the storm. Determined to ignore it, he pedals faster, but within seconds the tyre is completely deflated, rubbing against the tarmac with a loud squelching sound that could just as easily be his socks.

He calls Dave again, trying to shelter the phone inside the hood of his coat. 'How do I fix a flat tyre?' he says.

'Do you have a puncture repair kit?'

'Well, let's assume that I don't.'

'Then you need to take the bike to a shop.'

'Dave, there aren't even any trees around here, let alone a bloody shop.'

Lightning flashes overhead. Moments later, thunder rumbles through the rain.

'Is that what I think it is?' says Dave, sounding worried now. 'You shouldn't be out in a thunderstorm.'

'Then tell you what, I'll use my jet pack to fly to safety.'

'I'm not kidding, Ben.'

'Neither am I. If you could see where I am, you'd realize there is nowhere to go.' There's another flash and a loud clap of thunder, but Ben barely even hears it, his head too full of angry thoughts. 'Do you want to know the worst thing about all of this? I thought this trip was a way of earning my granddad's respect at last, and instead it's just confirmed that I'm a total loser.'

'That's not what your granddad thinks of you.'

'Dave, he barely speaks to me.'

'He's a man of few words.'

'It's been eighteen years.' Yet more lightning, the thunder following so fast and so loud, even Ben jumps. He stares up at the sky, angrier than ever. 'It's bloody perfect, isn't it? As if the whole trip wasn't already a fur-lined rat's fuck, now I'm going to get struck by lightning too. I'm going to die. In the rain. In… I don't even know where I am. If it wasn't for your GPS thing, they probably wouldn't find my body for years.'

'You shouldn't be using a phone, mate. Not in a thunder-storm.'

'But Dave—'

'I'm hanging up, for your sake. Call me when you get to safety.'

The line goes dead before Ben can ask what 'safety' might mean in a landscape like this. To the sound of yet more thunder, Ben starts pushing the bike, the flat tyre making it heavy and unwieldy. Off to the right, across the vast open flatlands, he notices a few rooftops, the merest suggestion of a village, but there's a channel of water between them, too wide to cross, and no bridge in sight. Too fed up even to complain about this, he walks in silence, nothing to interrupt his thoughts but the sound of the rain and the flat tyre. Moments later, there's a brilliant flash of light and a loud bang, a fork of lightning punching into a field just a few hundred yards off.

Ben stands there, dazed, staring at the spot long after the sound of thunder has rumbled away. Finally, he shouts into the rain. 'That's it, I've had enough! Enough of this rain, enough of this bloody lightning, and…' He looks down at his bike, at this deformed imitation of a proper ride. 'And I have definitely had enough of you.' He drags it towards the water, walking with a renewed sense of purpose. Up ahead, rain dances on the surface; a pockmarked veneer on dark, hidden depths. He picks up the bike as he reaches the water's edge. '*This* is what I think of cycling,' he yells, tossing the bike into the canal. With a splash unworthy of the occasion, it disappears from view, leaving Ben standing there, nothing but tired legs and sodden boots to carry him onwards.

Mayfair, London W1

It's obvious to Alice that she can't be around Piers, at least not for the next few days. It's true that he's been avoiding her since their little chat this morning, but in such a pronounced, circumspect manner, he may as well call a staff meeting and tell everyone what's going on. *I tried to have sex with Alice. She said no.*

Under the circumstances, there's only one thing for it…

Checklist:

   1. Look pale.

   2. Shiver.

   3. Groan occasionally.

It strikes Alice that this is yet further proof of what a good employee she is: the lengths she will go to in order to justify some sick leave; not the offhand, half-baked gestures of her colleagues, but rather a full theatrical performance. In the name of having no appetite, she's already eaten her lunch in the ladies' toilets, chewing only in the brief moments when someone flushed in the neighbouring cubicle.

Sitting at her desk now, she tries to think pale thoughts, willing herself to visibly blanche. Having attempted to *shiver* and failed, she pulls on her coat and flicks up the collar. She's wondering whether to put on a scarf too when Geneva appears, scrutinizing her from a safe distance. 'Are you all right?'

Alice pulls her coat closer, summons her weakest voice. 'I'm fine.'

'That's clearly not true, is it? You're looking a bit… sweaty, and off.' She backs away. 'To be honest, I've been thinking that about you all week. And I notice you spent a lot of time in the toilets today.' She retreats behind her desk. 'You should go home.'

'I can't do that,' replies Alice. 'There's still so much to do on the media pack.'

'God, is everyone this dreary in your gene pool? It's only work, Alice. It's hardly a matter of great importance.' She starts tapping at her keyboard. 'Shoo,' she says, not even looking up. 'And don't even think about coming back until you're fit as a fiddle.'

By the time Alice is shuffling towards the lift, her coat pulled tight about her, she has dedicated so much energy to trying to look sick, she starts to wonder if she really might be coming down with something. In the final moments before the doors open, Piers joins her.

'Before you go,' he says, 'I just want to say that I've done nothing wrong.'

'I thought we were going to forget it happened.'

'We are, but I can tell you're judging me.'

'You propositioned me.'

'I'm human.'

'And married. And my boss.'

'But there's no law against it, Alice. In fact, what could be more normal and healthy than a man being honest with a woman?' With a *ding*, the lift arrives and Alice shuffles inside. Piers moves closer, holds the door. 'And it's obvious that this other guy, whatever his name is. The *vegan*. It's obvious that he's completely wrong for you.' For a couple of seconds he stands there looking more hopeful, as if his words may have unlocked her heart. 'I don't even mind that you're fat. Doesn't that count for something?'

'Piers, please let go of the door.'

Crestfallen, he starts to back away, calling to her as the doors slide shut. 'If nothing else, Alice, at least remember this. I like bacon too.'

The Fens, south Lincolnshire
106 miles from Alice

It's late afternoon by the time Ben reaches shelter, his boots caked with mud from unofficial shortcuts across open fields. He takes refuge in the village pub, gently steaming in front of the log fire. It's only now that the drama is over that he ponders what he's done: that in the middle of a long bike ride, he's not just thrown away his bike, he's thrown away *Dave's* bike.

The woman from behind the bar approaches with two plates of cake, hands him one. 'Here, I made it myself.' Uninvited, she takes a seat beside him. 'The Nazis at Weight Watchers don't like me to eat this kind of thing on my own.' She takes a forkful, gasps. 'God, I needed that.' She takes another, appearing more relaxed with every chew. 'You look very damp.'

'I spent a long time in the rain.'

'That tends to do it,' she replies, still eating.

'I was on a charity bike ride,' he says, hoping to get the same reaction as he did with Janet. 'To Scotland.'

The woman looks unmoved. 'You say "was"?'

'Well, the bike's, er, sort of broken.'

'And you're not really dressed for a bike ride, are you? Don't they normally wear Lycra?'

'If you'd seen my bike, you'd realize that I already looked like a bell-end. I didn't need to flash one too.'

'Dear God, that icing she replies, through a full mouth. 'I can tell you now, a man's never brought me that kind of pleasure.' She takes another forkful. 'Did you start your ride at Land's End?'

'London.'

'Isn't Land's End the usual choice for charity?'

'Only if you're going to John O'Groats.'

'True, and that would just be overkill, wouldn't it? It's enough to do *something* for charity, you don't need to crucify yourself for them as well.' She gestures at the empty room. 'That's what this place is, a crucifixion. Everyone's always saying "Oh, you run a pub! How wonderful!", as though we spend all day just sitting around chatting with the punters.' Another mouthful of cake. 'The honest truth is, it's like being nailed to a big wooden cross and left to die.'

'Is business not too good?' says Ben, beginning to feel that he should take a bite of cake out of solidarity.

'It's not the business that's the problem. It's the chain that owns the place. A big parasitic leech that sucks out all the money, and I'm left with what? A blocked toilet and a urinal covered in puke. How's the cake?' Ben nods, his mouth full. 'If you find a little cat hair in there, please don't hold it against me. We seem to live in such a cloud of the stuff, it's a wonder the cat has any fur left.' She takes another bite. 'Though, just to put your mind at rest, it never seems to do the cat any harm. She's constantly bringing the stuff up.'

Ben is still sitting there, trying not to swallow, when his phone starts to ring. His first thought is that it must be Dave; that maybe the GPS chip is capable of informing him that his bike now sits in ten feet of brackish water. It's only when he checks the caller display that he sees it's not Dave at all.

'Sorry,' he says, washing the cake down with a large glug of beer, 'it's my gran. I should take this.'

He waits for her to leave, but she just gives him a smile and keeps eating. 'Don't mind me,' she says. 'I've got my cake to keep me occupied. I could happily sit here all day.'

Ben answers the call. 'Hello, Gran.'

'Benjamin,' she replies, her voice sounding smaller and more fragile than before. 'Is that you?'

'Gran? Are you all right? Is it Neville again?'

'No, no,' she replies, her voice beginning to fade. 'It's your grandfather. He's dead.'

Maidstone, Kent

42 miles from Alice

The funeral arrangements fall into place with all the speed of ordering a pizza, such is the ease with which we can pass from this life to the next. Ben hadn't thought of it until now, the way in which his grandparents' lives had been so small for so many years, with distant acquaintances rather than friends, and no family to speak of except for him. It's striking how much his grandmother appears to have aged since he saw her just last week, and even Neville seems a changed man, sitting in an uncharacteristic silence, perhaps aware that the world around him has shifted in fundamental ways. He stares at Ben with the same bulging eye as ever, but it's different now: the cockiness of earlier times replaced with a fear that Ben's never seen before.

'He's still not himself,' says Ben's grandmother, pouring them both a cup of tea.

'Do you think he'll be okay?'

'Things aren't going to be the same anymore. We all have to accept that.' She leans back in her armchair, appears dwarfed by it now. 'You probably don't know this, but Neville was your grandfather's idea. He thought it might break the ice a little for you, make the house a noisier, more boisterous place.'

'It certainly made it noisier.'

His grandmother stares into her tea, appears to find the words difficult. 'We wanted to bring some life into the house, you see. Something we should have done a long, long time before.' She looks up at him, eyes full of sadness. 'We realized that perhaps we'd made some bad decisions over the years. That maybe life would have worked out differently, if only we'd been a little different too.'

Behind them, Neville squawks half-heartedly. She turns and looks at him with soft, misty eyes, obviously seeing in this mad, deranged bird an opportunity to be a parent all over again; a second chance to get things right. 'I'll be sad to leave him.'

Ben chokes on his tea. 'What are you talking about?'

'I can't take him into the old people's home with me.'

'What old people's home? *This* is your home.'

'Oh, Benjamin, I can't stay here alone.'

'You're not alone. I'm here.'

'Your grandfather and I made all the arrangements a couple of years ago. We have some money tucked away for it. And there's the house, of course. You'll have to look after the sale for me.' She gazes around the room. 'I'll be sad to go. In our own way, we were very happy here.'

'I can move in with you. We'll live here together.'

She gives him the same fond look he remembers from his childhood: when he once gave her a cake made from mud, or created a new cocktail for her made from sherry and baking soda. 'Benjamin, when I look around this house, I see sixty years of my life. So many memories crowded into one place.'

'Which is exactly why you should stay.'

'I can't,' she says. 'It all reminds me of him, you see. Suddenly it's all a reminder of what's gone.'

'But what about all your memories?'

'What really matters is up here.' She taps her head as she says it, but presumably sees Ben's fear that her mind is not the safest choice of storage. 'And anything I forget, well, that will just make the rest of my days lighter, won't it?' She gives him a sad smile. 'Maybe one of these days I'll become so light, I'll just float away like a balloon.'

Feltham, West London

It's the sound of the front door slamming that wakes Alice; the sound of Mei leaving to do whatever it is that she does each day – allegedly studying for her degree, but who's to know for sure? It's already mid-morning, and the flat is so quiet it's impossible to imagine that life in London is already in full swing: millions of people crowded on top of one another; inching their way along busy streets; hurtling through cramped tunnels deep beneath the city.

Lying there, it seems that the world has moved on without her; that by pretending to be sick, by choosing to stay in bed, she hasn't simply rejected the day, she's rejected life itself.

When a text message arrives from Rachel, she doesn't even read it; doesn't care to hear what new hopes and fears Rachel has invented today. But just a couple of minutes later, the phone starts ringing and it seems impossible to ignore it.

Alice doesn't have a chance to speak before Rachel's voice comes rushing down the line. 'Are you okay? I texted you, but I didn't hear anything.'

'You texted me two minutes ago.'

'And that's not enough time to reply?'

'It's, er, been a really busy morning. Non-stop.' She glances around her room, the only movement coming from dust motes in the sunshine. 'And I'm about to go into a meeting.'

'With your boss?'

'That's right.'

'The one that tried to seduce you?'

'Rachel…'

'Sorry, you probably can't talk, can you? Are you with him now?'

149

'Something like that.'

'I was just calling to say that I've uploaded a new video to my channel.' She seems to hesitate a moment, perhaps waiting for Alice to express her excitement. 'Let me know what you think. It's already getting attention. I've texted you the link.'

'Sure, I'll take a look later,' says Alice, already hoping that a meteor might wipe out mankind before she needs to give Rachel her opinion. 'Look, I need to go.'

'Please feel free to give the video a thumb's up. And if you want to leave a comment, that'd be great too. Something like "Wow, this is better than Beyoncé", that kind of thing.'

'Sorry, I have to go now.'

The guilt kicks in as soon as she's hung up; as if it's not enough that she's skipping work on the pretence of being sick, now she's lying to her best friend too. Hoping to atone in some way for her shortcomings as a human being, she checks Rachel's new video, her heart sinking yet further as she realizes that Rachel's chosen to sing this one a cappella. With no music for her voice to hide behind, the video is much like watching an orphan gazelle wander alone in the African bush, every passing second a reminder that this cannot end well.

'I can't do this,' she says, stopping the video just as Rachel takes a loud, deep breath in preparation for a high note. Turning her phone off, she sinks back into her pillows, setting herself adrift on a sea of sloth. And although it occurs to her that she should be worried by this – that she's too young and too educated to simply give up – she knows that this is precisely where she will stay, the entire day stretching out ahead of her, full of nothing but her own sad thoughts.

Maidstone, Kent
42 miles from Alice

'It's funny,' says Ben, as he shows Dave through to the living room, 'everything in the house looks the same, but it feels like a different world.'

'How's your gran coping?'

He lowers his voice. 'She was up earlier, getting the under-taker sorted and all that stuff, but she's gone back to bed now. Says she just wants to be alone.'

'And how are you doing?'

'I'm a bit dazed, to be honest. It's like everything I thought I knew has been swept away. The funeral's going to be next Tuesday, and then she's moving straight into the old people's home. I've got to get this whole place packed up and...' He sighs. 'I don't even know where to start. She's not taking much with her, and let's be realistic, how much can I fit in our place?'

'Please tell me you're not taking the piano.'

'That bloody thing. Do you know it's never once been played the entire time I've lived in this house?'

'You could have learnt to play it.'

'I wanted to, but that's the point, no one's *allowed* to touch it. Even my gran only goes near it with a duster. And as you can tell, not a lot of dusting goes on in this house.'

Dave wanders over to Neville's cage, the two of them peering at one another in silence. 'He's very subdued, isn't he?'

'She wants me to take him.'

'You? She wants *you* to have Neville?'

'That was my reaction too. How do you feel about living with a parrot?'

'I wouldn't mind,' he replies, looking uneasy now. 'Though, I do want to talk about that.'

'About Neville?'

'No, about living together.' He looks unsure how to go on. 'The thing is, I've been seeing Agnes.'

'Seeing her?'

'Yes, mate. *Seeing* her.'

'Naked, you mean? Putting your bits in each other?'

'Well, if you must put it that way, yes.'

'I suddenly feel a bit sick.'

'See, I knew you'd say that, and it was just a casual thing, which is why I never told you before.' He hesitates again. 'But the thing is, it's all changed in the last few days.'

'Trust me, I know about things changing.'

'Mate, she's pregnant. And we both want to keep it.'

*

Ben's shock at the news is made ten times worse by the need to be quiet for his grandmother's sake. Whereas he might otherwise have jumped around the room swearing loudly, he has to sit there, eyes wide, trying to come to terms with it all.

'If it's doing *your* head in,' says Dave, 'imagine how *I* feel.'

'You're going to be a *dad*.'

'Don't. Even the word scares me. I feel like I should start wearing tweed and smoking a pipe.'

'Imagine if it grows up to be a smackhead or something.'

'Thank you, Ben. One more thing to worry about.'

'And with *Agnes*.' He shakes his head, still in shock. 'I never saw that coming.'

'You didn't think it strange that she used to come over so much?'

'To help you make candles, not to, you know… light your wick. So I guess you'll be moving into her place?'

'Eventually, but we can discuss all that once you're back in London.'

'But we may as well discuss it now, don't you think? I may as well know what I'm dealing with.'

'I'd love to keep living with you, honestly. And I'll keep paying my share of the rent until you find someone else.'

And though Ben wants to tell him that he'll never be able to find someone else – that no one could take Dave's place because he's the best friend that Ben's ever had – instead he just nods. 'It's all right,' he says. 'We'll figure it out.'

The 10:35 to Wickford, Essex

It's not a train ride, it's an exercise in guilt: pondering the fact that she should be at work rather than speeding away from London; that she should be grazing on an apple rather than chewing through a large jam doughnut. It's only as Alice reaches her parents' house that it occurs to her that maybe she really is unwell after all: for the first time in her adult life, she has gone there uninvited; she has put herself, *by choice*, in a position where her mother can spend the rest of the day criticizing her weight and asking inappropriate questions.

She's nearing the front door when she hears the music from inside: the relentless drum beats of a samba, and the sound of laughter too. It's so unexpected, so out of place, she stops to make sure that she has the right house. She's still standing there, confused, when her mother opens the front door, a large cocktail in her hand, and a green and yellow party hat sitting askew on her head. 'Alice?' she shouts over the music. 'What are you doing here?'

'Is this a bad time?'

'Well, you could have given us some warning,' she says, ushering Alice inside. 'We're having a little taste of Brazil.' She holds up her cocktail. 'Would you like a cai... cai-piranha?'

'It's not even twelve. Isn't it a bit early to be drinking?'

'And aren't you a bit too young to be asking questions like that?' She shakes her glass. 'There is fruit in it, darling. It probably counts as one of my five a day.' She sashays towards the music. 'Come and meet our guests.'

Alice follows the sound of music and laughter into the living room, finds her father – no longer in exile in the attic – dancing with another couple of a similar age, everyone clearly too drunk to care that Alice is staring at them, open-mouthed.

'This is our daughter, the party police,' shouts her mother.

The other woman shrieks with laughter. 'Someone in this family needs to be sensible,' she says to Alice. 'Lord knows your parents can be very naughty.'

Unsure how to respond, Alice just gives her a polite smile.

'You definitely need a drink,' says her mother, leaving the room.

Alice follows her out to the kitchen. 'This isn't quite what I'd expected to find.'

'Are we not allowed to entertain without your permission?' She fumbles with some wedges of lime, clumsily putting them in a glass with a few spoonfuls of sugar. She dumps in some ice cubes, several of them missing the glass completely. 'Dennis and Anita were in Brazil last year,' she says, filling the glass to the brim with cachaca, and handing it to Alice. 'They're showing us how to have some fun, Latino-style.'

'I've never heard you mention them before.'

'Well, we've only got to know them recently. But they're very nice people.' She blushes. 'Dennis is quite handsome, don't you think?'

*

Given how drunk everyone is by one o'clock in the afternoon, it's probably for the best that Alice's mother doesn't try to cook. Instead, they all sit around the dining table, eating by the fistful from communal bowls of nuts and crisps.

'This isn't how they do it in Brazil,' says Anita.

'What do they eat there?' says Alice's mother.

Anita looks to Dennis for inspiration, but he just shrugs. 'To be honest,' she says, 'I found it to be more of a calories-from-alcohol kind of place. There's no need to eat.'

158

Alice's mother takes another mouthful of nuts. 'How's Ben?' she says, the words coming at Alice on an odorous wave of peanut and tiny specks of saliva. Not waiting for a response, she turns to their guests. 'It's such a shame she couldn't bring him too. He's a lovely young man. An engineer.'

'You don't know him,' says Alice. 'You've never met him.'

'But sometimes you can just tell, can't you?' She speaks to the table again. 'Fingers crossed, we might actually be grandparents after all.'

'Mother, I think I can safely say that a family is not on the cards.'

'Ignore her,' she says, to the rest of the table. 'She's always wanted children.'

'That's not true,' replies Alice.

'Nonsense, you did nothing but talk about it when you were young.'

'When I was four years old, perhaps.'

'I remember you used to play with your dolls all the time.'

'I tied one to a balloon and watched it drift out to sea. I buried another in the garden.'

'Well, I think it's exactly what this family needs,' says her mother, raising her glass. 'To grandchildren. A new generation.'

Alice's father naturally embraces the toast, raising his glass so enthusiastically, he spills some of it. 'To Ben, to Alice, to family, and to new beginnings for us all.'

'Grandchildren *are* a wonderful thing,' says Anita. 'I can't imagine life without ours.'

Alice's mother appears irritated by the comment, her mood visibly souring. She turns to Alice again. 'And how's work?'

'Not great, in all honesty.'

Her mother rests her hand on hers, a rare gesture of maternal warmth. 'Alice, darling, no one likes a whiner.'

'You did ask.'

'And I don't think I ever will again, because you never seem to have a good word to say about it.'

'Do you not care why?'

'Not really. Contrary to what you young people seem to think, life isn't one long party.'

'My boss has been making sexual advances.'

The table goes silent.

'Well,' says her mother, finally, 'it could be good for your career.'

'Mother, you're not supposed to say that.'

'Why not? You're always complaining about how little you earn, and yet then when the Good Lord shows you a way...'

'What about my rights as a woman? About feminism?'

'Don't lecture me on that. I think you'll find I'm the ultimate feminist, thank you very much. I didn't have you until I was thirty-eight years old.' She turns to Dennis. 'I was pursuing my career.'

'You were a receptionist,' says Alice.

'It was still a job. Does a woman have to be a rocket scientist to have value? I don't think a twenty-two-year-old, who by the way has been given everything in life, can talk to *me* about feminine empowerment.'

'My point was equality. Women not *needing* to prove anything because we're all equal.'

'Oh please, the world gave up all that nonsense in the seventies. I hope you won't be filling your children's heads with stuff like that.'

Alice's father raises his glass again. 'Alice, I have no doubt that you and Ben will be very happy together. It's a new chapter in your life and I just want to say we're here for you.' The words come so heavy with emotion, it's hard to tell if he's speaking from the heart or is simply drunk. 'We're here to support you, Alice, I want you to remember that. Anytime you need us, we're here for you.'

Maidstone, Kent
23 miles from Alice

After a long morning of sifting through the chaos of his grandparents' lives, Ben takes a break in his grandfather's armchair, the first time in his life that he's ever dared to sit there.

It's only once he's seated that he realizes it's in the perfect defensive position, a sniper's nest, everything in clear view. Ben wonders if that's what was going through his grandfather's mind for all those years: keeping on the lookout; forever poised to defend the family home.

Next to the chair, the shelves are still stacked with his grandfather's books. There's one in particular that he seemed to read and re-read, often sitting there with it open in his hands. Ben takes it from the shelf, tries to feel the weight of its history; the binding worn thin, the gilded lettering of the title long since rubbed from view. Even the cover has a warmth to it, as though his grandfather has only just put it down.

He turns to the first page, but it doesn't fall open with the ease of a well-read book. He looks up to find his grandmother watching him.

'You seem disappointed,' she says.

'It looks well-thumbed, but it doesn't feel like it.'

'Did you never wonder why he was always holding that book? And always at the same page?'

Ben flicks deeper, the book yielding to him now, falling open on a page that his grandfather must have looked at a thousand times. And there, nestled against the stitching, a photograph of Ben. Transfixed, he picks it up and peers closer. He looks so young, it was surely taken in the first few months of his new life with them. He's sitting on a park bench, staring at the camera with a serious expression. And on either side of him, his grandparents, trying for all the world to look happy, despite everything they'd just lost.

'Come with me,' she says, holding out her hand. 'There's something he wanted you to have.'

They walk hand in hand across the living room, past a sullen-looking Neville, and out to the hallway. When they reach her bedroom, she takes a small box from one of the dresser drawers and hands it to him. 'He told me to give you this, when the time came.' Ben holds it in his hands, feels how its outer covering has softened with age. 'There's nothing to be frightened of, darling. Open it.'

He swings back the lid, his jaw dropping as the contents come into view: a military medal, nestled in a bed of silk.

'He was a prisoner of war in Korea. The communists held him for almost two years. Starved and tortured, the lot...'

'But why did he never tell me?'

'He wasn't one for attention, especially when he had friends who never made it back.' She smiles at the medal, at this legacy of a brave man. 'He'd seen some awful things out there. He didn't think a child should know what a terrible place the world can be.'

'And he wanted *me* to have it?'

'You sound surprised.'

'I... I didn't even know he liked me.'

'Benjamin, your grandfather wasn't a man who could tell others how he felt. Couldn't tell me, sometimes couldn't even tell himself. But I could understand all the things he didn't know how to say. That's what it means to love someone, you see...' Her words drift into silence and, for a few moments, Ben assumes that she's lost her train of thought, but then she's looking at him again through rheumy eyes. 'We were like two pieces of a jigsaw puzzle, he and I; we couldn't have fitted together with anyone else. And now he's gone, the picture will always be incomplete.'

The 18:26 to London Liverpool Street

It's already dark by the time Alice nears London, the city seeming to swell and thicken around her as the train passes through Stratford, the financial district rearing up in the distance, a high-rise forest of lights shining against the night sky. After spending time with her parents, there's normally a sense of relief at this point, but today it feels more profound than that: like she's seen something that should have remained hidden; that the parents she's just left behind in Essex are not the same people she thought she knew.

Looking out the window, she ponders that elsewhere in this city Geneva is leaving the office with Harry, that Piers is finding new ways to avoid his wife, and that Ben is... She stops herself, already embarrassed at how much she's trafficked in him over the last two weeks; how she's taken a sweet, guileless young man and spun him into a fiction to suit her own needs.

Wanting to make amends – feeling that she must, in fact, create a new narrative, not just for her own sake, but Ben's too – she makes a phone call, certain that it's the right thing to do; certain that she is, in some small way, shifting her life in a better and healthier direction.

'Frida, it's me, Alice. If it's not too late to accept your invitation, I'd love to come to the party tomorrow.'

Maidstone, Kent

42 miles from Alice

Time moves differently in this house. Ben's only been back for a couple of days and already it feels like he's been there for ever; that he may, in fact, be a five-year-old boy all over again, trapped there for another decade or two.

Despite Neville's occasional squawks, the silence of the house puts Ben in an introspective mood. As he did so many times as a child, he stands in front of the hallway mirror, gazing at his reflection, trying to divine something new about his origins.

Inevitably his grandmother joins him, watching as he peers at himself.

'Do I really have my father's chin?' he asks her.

Even in her grief, his grandmother still manages a smile at a question she's heard countless times before. 'Yes, I think you do.' She stares at him, perhaps trying to imagine that this is not her grandchild at all, but rather her young son come home at last. 'Though, of course,' she says, her smile fading, 'I can't be certain. He was barely out of his teens the last time we saw him. And with all the photos gone...'

Ben turns back to his reflection, standing so close to the mirror now that he can see every detail. 'Do you think my mother's eyes were like mine?'

'I wish I knew, Benjamin. I wish we'd been allowed to meet

her.' She begins to wander away, calling to him as she goes. 'We should keep packing.'

Ben follows her through to the living room. 'Have you decided what you'll be taking?'

'I think my new room will be too small to take much.' She stands there, amid the accumulated junk of half a century. 'It's a good opportunity for a bit of a clear out, isn't it?'

'What about the piano?'

'I used to love playing it.'

'Then why did you stop?'

'Oh, Benjamin, life can be complicated.' She moves closer to the piano, but remains at arm's length, almost appears afraid of it. 'I taught your father to play on it. And he was good at it, too; he was playing constantly as a child. But after he left, and then with everything that happened, even the sound of it brought back too many memories.' She finally reaches across, rests a thin, frail hand on the lid. 'We spent years telling ourselves that it was still a valuable possession, that it was an important thing to keep. To be honest, I would have taken an axe to it long before now, but there was your grandfather…' She falls silent, looks confused. 'What were we saying?'

'About taking an axe to the piano.'

'Don't be mad, Benjamin, what would your grandfather say?'

'Well, I can't take it.'

She crosses to Neville's cage, speaks with her back to Ben. 'I leave it in your hands, Benjamin. Whatever you decide is fine by me.'

'I found a box of old bus tickets this morning. From the sixties. I'm assuming you don't want those either?'

She turns to look at him, appears confused again. 'What's that, darling?'

'I'm going to look through everything, but most of it's just going to be thrown away.'

She shrugs, turns back to Neville. 'That's the story of life itself, isn't it? All good things come to an end sooner or later.'

Notting Hill, London W11

Given Frida's strident political views, not to mention her dress sense, it seems reasonable to anticipate that she lives in an air of dereliction; if not an actual squat then at least a messy flat that aspires to be one; an unkempt rejection of capitalist values. It comes as a surprise, then, to find that she lives in a stuccoed house on one of Notting Hill's better streets.

The contradiction is clearly not lost on Frida. 'As you can see, we're sleeping with the enemy,' she says, ushering Alice indoors. 'Though all the better to see what's wrong with society. We're on the frontlines here, that's for sure. Only the other day, someone across the road bought a *Range Rover*.' She says the words with such disgust, anyone would think it akin to child pornography. 'I have to restrain myself from going over there and saying it's people like them who are bringing the world to its knees.'

Spent by her hatred of other people's prosperity, she appears to lose interest in any further conversation, instead just leading Alice through to the crowded drawing room.

'What shall I do with this?' says Alice, holding up a cake tin.

'You can pop it on the table over there,' replies Frida, hovering in the background as Alice pries it open and lifts out a fruitcake.

'It *is* vegan,' says Alice. 'Organic, too. No nasty pesticides to kill all those lovely insects.'

Frida nevertheless looks suspicious. 'Can you tell me exactly what's in it?'

'It's basically a very rich fruitcake,' says Alice, still beaming at the thought of her handiwork.

'No eggs?'

'Of course not. No eggs, no dairy. No meat! In fact, to keep with the natural theme, I even sweetened it with honey.' The room becomes quieter. 'It was *organic* honey,' she adds, aware that everyone is now staring at her.

'Which is nevertheless an *animal* product,' says Frida, already putting the cake back in its tin. 'I'll give you a leaflet later about the evils of beekeeping. You'll never want to touch the stuff again.' Since Alice is already craving a sausage roll, this seems unlikely. Thankfully Frida has turned her attention elsewhere, calling to a young man on the far side of the room. 'Chris…'

Alice expects someone in a grubby Baja hoodie, someone with the air of a small-time drug smuggler, but it's actually a clean-cut young man who approaches. Perhaps in his late twenties, he has a gentle smile, a generous waistline, and messy blond hair suggestive of long hours spent lazing in bed. She's still admiring him when she realizes that Frida is talking, standing between them like a referee.

'… as you can tell, she's a fixer-upper—' She turns to Alice. 'Purely in a vegan sense, of course.' Back to Chris, '… but she has excellent potential and I think you're the man.'

With that she walks away, leaving them face to face while Alice desperately tries not to say the first words that come to mind. *I hear your brother's just got out of prison. Are the showers really as bad as they say?*

It's Chris who speaks first. 'So,' he says, glancing at her shoes, 'you volunteer at the kitchen?'

'Yes,' replies Alice, also checking her shoes: leather flats, each festooned with a leather tassel, as though wanting to maximize every opportunity for animal slaughter. Self-conscious now, she begins to talk more quickly. 'To be fair, Frida is much, much more dedicated than me.' She glances at her shoes again. 'As you can probably tell, my life has basically been a twenty-two-year orgy of ecological destruction. I probably have the carbon footprint of a small nation. And don't even get me started on the importance of bacon.'

As Chris stares back at her, she realizes that maybe this wasn't the best thing to say at a party of vegan environmentalists.

'You have very beautiful eyes,' is all he says. 'I like the way they sparkle when you speak.'

'When I'm busy putting my foot in it, you mean.'

He lowers his voice. 'You've not mentioned Frida's house. I'd call you the very soul of discretion.'

Alice lowers her voice too. 'Well, I *was* wondering.'

He glances around, as if even discussing this is a treasonable offence. 'Trust fund,' he says, mouthing the words with barely a whisper.

'No!' says Alice, shocked.

And now it's Chris whose eyes are sparkling. 'I think we need to get you a drink,' he says, his smile suggesting that this is only the first salvo in a long evening of shameless flirtation.

Maidstone, Kent

42 miles from Alice

Ben wakes up to find Neville's cage empty, the patio doors wide open, and the garden drenched in rain.

'I wanted to let him choose whether to live with you or not,' says his grandmother, staring out at the downpour.

'Gran, this isn't the Congo. He can't survive in this climate.'

'But he still deserves a choice, don't you think?'

'Where is he?'

'Out there, in the tree.'

At first, Ben can only see wet leaves, but then he spots him: sitting on a lower branch of the oak tree, looking damp and grief-stricken, much the way Ben has felt for the last few days.

'He's always wanted to go outside,' says his grandmother. 'Though I doubt this is how he expected it to be.'

'Should I go and get him?'

'No, no, he needs to make up his own mind.'

'But we're supposed to be going out in a while.'

'We'll just leave the door open.'

'We can't do that!'

'Why? You're worried that someone may break in and steal everything? That would surely save us the trouble of sorting through it all.'

★

In polite terms, their visit to the nursing home is a getting-to-know-you, a chance for everyone to have a cup of tea and some cake, and pretend to be excited at the prospect of institutionalized care; a neatly furnished, well-fed pathway ending in death. Ben has already decided what the staff will be like: smiling a little too much, like cult members trying to put their best face forward. *See, we're not creepy and abusive. We're normal people, just like you.*

They ride over there in silence, Ben sitting in the front seat of the taxi, marvelling at how much can change in the space of just a few days. A mere week ago, his grandparents were living together in the house where he grew up, and yet now his grandfather is dead and his grandmother is on the cusp of moving into an old people's home. He glances at her on the back seat, worried that she, too, may be feeling overwhelmed by it all, but there's an air of resignation about her, as if she'd long since prepared herself for this moment.

As they pull up in front of the building, Ben turns to her again. 'Even once you've moved in here, you can call me any time you like. Not just to come and visit you, but to take you out and do things. We can go on some daytrips together.'

'Dearest Benjamin, you're always so sweet.'

He helps her from the car, steeling himself for the abject misery they'll surely find inside: old people tied to armchairs, the air thick with the stench of boiled cabbage and rotting corpses.

What he finds is more like a cruise ship, as though the whole building may up anchor at any moment and drift away to the Caribbean: residents are playing cards and board games, even dancing. A smiling nurse leads them through this carnival scene. 'We can already show you the room where you'll be living. And then you're just in time to join us for lunch.'

Ben's grandmother gives his hand a squeeze. 'Come and see my room with me, but don't feel obliged to stay.'

'I'm not leaving you alone.'

'Benjamin, it's only for a few hours. And anyway, I'm not alone.' She smiles at her new surroundings. 'I suspect I'll never be alone again.'

★

Neville is back in his cage when Ben returns home, the outside world evidently having lost its appeal. Seeing Neville like this, sitting in a chastened silence, Ben decides that perhaps they could be kindred spirits after all: two people who've learnt the hard way that life does not always work out how we expect.

His head cocked to one side, Neville watches Ben approach. They stare at one another, two survivors amid the wreckage of life gone wrong.

'It's just you and me now, isn't it?' says Ben. Neville remains motionless, one bulging eye staring straight up at him. 'You're coming to London with me and…' Even in the spirit of their *entente cordiale*, Ben struggles to say the words. 'And I'm going to look after you.'

Deciding this is the right moment for a grand gesture, he puts his hand into the cage.

Neville stares at it, doubtless as perplexed as Ben by the rapid shift in their relationship.

'It's okay,' says Ben. 'I'm your friend.'

This seems to be the cue that Neville has been waiting for. Beak wide open, he lunges for Ben's finger. Ben snatches his hand away barely in time, locking the cage as Neville begins to squawk so loudly, so shrilly, it's easy to imagine that every window in the house will start to explode.

'You child of Satan,' says Ben, backing away from the cage.

Still screaming, Neville leaps against the bars, snapping at Ben with a beak that longs for the taste of blood and bone.

Ben hurries into the spare room, picks up one of the many blankets that are waiting to be packed away, returns to the pandemonium of the living room.

'I think you need to take a nap,' he says, scarecely able to hear himself. With a toss and a flip of the wrist, the blanket takes flight.

Stunned into silence now, Neville watches as the woollen canopy descends from above, engulfing his cage and blocking the world from view.

Acton, London W3

Other than the usual pleasantries – thanking Frida for the party, and telling her what a nice time she had – Alice has tried to avoid conversation since she arrived; avoided even looking at Frida, lest she says all the questions screaming inside her head. *House? Notting Hill? TRUST FUND?*

She steals a surreptitious glance at Frida on the other side of the room, grimacing as she stirs a large pot of something meaty. Quickly looking away, Alice busies herself with a mental list, anything to keep her mind distracted.

On the menu today:

1. Tomato soup.

Alice peers into the large pot of viscous, orange-red gunk in front of her, certain that it contains many things, but tomatoes are probably not one of them.

Again, another furtive glance at Frida.

2. Penne in a mystery sauce.

Alice knows there's bacon in it, simply because Frida asked her to chop it, but once that was done, she insisted on doing the rest herself. Knowing Frida and her dislike of waste, it's easy to believe that she's used everything donated by the supermarket, regardless of merit; can easily imagine her tipping a jar of raspberry jam in there, purely in the name of environmental responsibility.

She glances at Frida yet again, their eyes meeting this time. Alice quickly looks away, tries even harder to concentrate on her list.

3. One packet of crisps per person (assorted flavours).

She can already anticipate the problems this will create: that at least a third of the people will be dissatisfied with the random choice of flavour they're given; these people who've been shafted by life now finding that they've been short-changed by the charity process too. And Alice, eager to preserve their last remaining shreds of dignity, will rummage through what's on offer to give them something they do like, until all she's left with is a box full of flavours that no one wants, and the people at the back of the queue – whose only sin was to come last – will have one more reason to think that the world is out to get them.

She makes a conscious effort not to look at Frida.

4. One chocolate bar each (hopefully two each for the kids).

She's imagining herself as a sort of Father Christmas, handing out sweeties to wide-eyed children, when Frida speaks. 'We may as well talk about it.'

'Excuse me?' replies Alice, hoping to sound naïve.

'I know it's confusing, but it's only half true that the house is mine. I inherited it, but…' She sighs, keeps stirring her pot of sauce. 'Let's just say my family doesn't approve of my lifestyle. It's in the terms of the trust that I'm not allowed to sell the house or even rent it out. And I'll be damned if I'm going to let yet another house sit empty in this city.'

Unsure if this is an actual invitation to dialogue or simply an anti-capitalist *mea culpa*, Alice tries to keep things light. 'Well, it's a lovely house.'

'No, it's not, it's a bourgeois prison. It's a constant reminder that all my family has ever cared about is money and prestige.

179

But the thing is, if I give it up, I lose everything else too. Income I can use to really help people. To make a difference.' She stirs the sauce again, but distractedly now, her mind else-where. 'There's just so much to be done, that's the thing. So many people who need help.'

'It sounds like a complicated family,' Alice replies. Frida says nothing, appears lost in her own thoughts. 'My family can be hard work as well. Though I wouldn't say no if they gave me somewhere to live. Not that that'd ever happen.' More silence. 'I saw them a couple of days ago, and they were acting very… I don't even know how to say it. They were just different somehow. I'm wondering if this is the right time to ask if they'd put a deposit on a flat for me. As a loan, of course; I'm not asking for hand-outs and freebies. I'm a little scared of asking, but there's no harm in trying my luck, surely?'

It's obvious that Frida hasn't listened to a word; that Alice could, in fact, say anything and still get no response. She's thinking of testing this theory – perhaps making some com-ments about flying elephants and alien abductions – when Frida finally speaks, still staring into the pot of sauce.

'I always think it's unfair how the poor get mocked for playing the lottery, because it's all a lottery, when you think about it: being born into a financially secure family, or having parents who nurture and encourage you, or simply having the skills and intelligence to figure a way out of it all. And if a person doesn't have any of those things, it's like society flicks them the finger and tells them that it's all their own fault.' For an instant, there's a look on her face that Alice hasn't seen before: the sadness of a woman who knows she can't change the world. Just as quickly, it passes. 'Could you have a taste of this for me? Tell me what you think?'

Alice crosses to the vat of mystery sauce. 'What's in it?' she says, as she takes a spoon.

'Oh, this and that,' replies Frida, with a shrug.

'Well, it smells good,' says Alice.

'It smells of bacon,' corrects Frida. 'Did you know that pigs and humans have almost identical DNA?' She watches as Alice blows on the mixture to cool it down. 'When you think about it,' she says, as Alice pops the sauce in her mouth, 'it's no different to eating your mother.'

Alice forces herself to swallow. 'It's lovely,' she says, but Frida looks unimpressed with the compliment. 'I mean, even without the bacon, it would be very tasty.'

'I sometimes dream of what would happen if we could serve a vegan menu.' *They would smash the place up*, thinks Alice. *They would point knives at us until they got meat.* 'Imagine the optimism, the vitality, if only we made everything plant-based. Chris can tell you more about that on your next date.'

Alice blushes. 'What makes you think we'll go on a date?'

For the first time this morning, Frida appears to relax. 'I may spend a lot of time talking about all the things that are wrong with the world, but even I can see when two people like each other.'

Mayfair, London W1

What I should be doing with my life...

Even as Alice writes the words, she knows the main thing she should be doing right now is paying attention to what's being said in the team meeting. One of her many Sloane colleagues is currently explaining something about canapés, but unless she's about to serve some to prove her point, Alice would rather not listen.

    1. **Find a new job.**

This seems so obvious, she scratches it out and starts again.

    2. **Volunteer in Africa.**

She's not so sure *what* she would do, or why the good people of Africa would be willing to suffer her doing it, but it feels *right* – something worthy to atone for all the other things she's not yet accomplished. Frida is sure to have some connections in Africa – though opportunities to blow up oil wells is not quite what Alice has in mind. She closes her eyes, imagines herself as a teacher, standing at the front of some thatched school hut, teaching children to read and write and dream big. But then reality cuts into the fantasy: the mental image of young girls asking Alice what *she* did with her university education. And what would she say then? That she became a poorly paid intern at a PR firm – a role in which her most important task was simply to say yes to everything, like some backstreet crack whore short of cash.

She crosses it out, starts again.

1. Learn the cello.

If nothing else, this seems an appropriate reaction to Mei and their upstairs neighbour: the cello's mournful quality expressing Alice's feelings about them more succinctly than words ever could, particularly when played badly at three in the morning. Though on that basis, perhaps the trumpet would be a better idea?

2. Learn to ride a unicycle.

It's a random thought that comes from nowhere, but it suddenly seems like the best idea she's ever had. It will be fun and inspiring – everything that she once expected her career to be – and a unicycle will surely be an amazing workout too? She can picture herself in the park every weekend, slowly growing more proficient, perhaps even becoming a familiar face to local joggers and young families: everyone smiling and applauding as she makes her umpteenth lap of the lake, juggling colourful balls as she goes.

'Alice?' She looks up, realizes that Piers and everyone else in the room is staring at her. 'Is everything okay?'

She clears her throat. 'I'm fine,' she replies, the words coming out in a cracked squeak.

'So, then, what's your answer?'

She hesitates, the eyes of the room on her; a time for her to draw on all her years of education.

'Sure,' she says, hopeful that she's struck a tone of quiet authority. 'It's a yes from me.'

Everyone looks pleased with her response, and for a few fleeting moments Alice imagines that she's a born leader, so good at her job she can function on autopilot, always able to say the right thing at the right time.

'Great,' says Piers, 'we look forward to eating it.'

Maidstone, Kent
34 miles from Alice

Until he's about to knock on the neighbour's front door, Ben thinks it's a good idea to offer these people something from his grandparents' house. They have, after all, known each other for many years; the whole street stuck in such a time warp, it remains a little slice of the nineties, all its pebble-dashed pretensions and bigotries preserved intact.

He notices the curtains move as he walks up the front path, but there's a long silence after he's rung the bell. Finally, a white-haired woman comes to the door. 'Benjamin,' she says, clearly unhappy to be disturbed. 'How can I help you?'

His reply comes out before he's had a chance to check himself. 'You're looking more and more like a man.'

She doesn't flinch; having lived there even longer than Ben, she's had sufficient time to grow accustomed to his ways, from the young boy who would scream in his sleep until the whole neighbourhood was awake, to the troubled teenager who would climb onto his grandparents' roof and refuse to come down, even when the fire brigade arrived.

'What is it you want?' she says, her voice more clipped now.

'My grandfather's dead.'

'Yes, I saw the undertakers. I'm sorry for your loss.'

'My gran is selling up. I just wanted to know if there's anything in the house you'd like.' She stares at him, as though he's just suggested that she can rummage through their bins. He can feel yet more words on his lips. *There's a parrot, too, if you want one*, but he keeps them in. 'The funeral is tomorrow, if you're free.'

187

'Oh, what a shame,' she replies, giving him a smile that even Ben can recognize as fake. 'I'm afraid we already have plans, but please give your grandmother my condolences.'

Ben scrutinizes her expression, becomes excited at his new-found understanding. 'My mate Dave's told me about that kind of smile. It means "Piss off, I hate you".'

'Goodbye, Benjamin,' she says, closing the door before he can say another word.

Mayfair, London W1

It's only as Alice and her colleagues are spilling from the meeting room that she's able to corral Lucy and quietly ask what happened in there.

'I know this will probably sound like a dumb question,' she says. 'I'm just wondering, what is it that I agreed to?'

Lucy appears relieved, lowers her voice. 'Did you do too much coke this morning as well?'

'No!' The moment begins to sour. 'What I mean,' she adds, hurriedly, 'is my drug of choice is…' *Coffee*, she wants to say, but decides this may lack the necessary camaraderie. 'You know, *other stuff…*'

'Silly me, I should have known. I suspect you smoke a fair bit, don't you? And then the munchies kick in.' She waits for one of their colleagues to pass. 'You're welcome to put some hash in the cake you've agreed to make.'

'Cake?'

'Yes, Piers thinks it would be a nice way of keeping every-one motivated. Every Tuesday, someone's going to bake a cake. And you're going first.'

Things to do:

1. **Never say yes unless you know what you're agreeing to.**
2. **Stop making lists.**

Back at her desk now, Alice mentally runs through all the cakes she'd happily make for herself, deciding each time that it's either too expensive or simply too good for these people. It doesn't help that she can already see how her colleagues will handle things when it's their turn: corralling maids and au pairs to make a cake for them, or simply ordering one from Fortnum's and removing the packaging on the way to the office.

She's so distracted that when her phone starts to ring, she simply answers it without even checking who it might be. 'Yes?' she says, doing nothing to hide her irritability.

'Good morning,' replies Chris. 'How are you today?'

'Chris!' she says, blushing at the mere sound of his voice, and panicking now that she's just answered his call sounding like a Russian prison guard. 'I didn't realize it was you. I, er… you caught me at a really bad moment.'

'Should I call back later?'

'No! Of course not. It was only a bad moment until you called and now…' *And now I'm talking too much.* 'What I'm trying to say is that it's still super busy here, but it's great to hear from you and…' *I'm still talking too much.* 'And so, er, yes, how are you?'

'I was hoping we could grab a drink later this week.'

'Sure, why not?' says Alice, hoping to sound offhand.

'I was thinking Wednesday.'

'Absolutely,' she replies, suddenly disappointed that he didn't suggest Friday or Saturday; already worried that maybe he has better things to do on those nights. 'Wednesday it is.'

The 08:05 to London Waterloo

Despite thinking that she should be making fewer lists, not more, the temptation is too great:

Three ways I'm going to make today a great day...

She tries not to sigh, aware that the day, at best, will be another test of endurance. Even now, barely past eight o'clock in the morning, she's already standing in a crowded railway carriage, trying to balance a cake tin in her hands as the train rocks and rattles its way towards London. She peers down at the tin, finds comfort in the thought of the Victoria sponge inside. It's true that she didn't like the idea of baking for her colleagues, but now that the task is finished, it feels right somehow, as if the act of feeding them cake might even transform them into better, sweeter people. If she'd had the money, she would have created something ten times more elaborate; a rich Christmas cake, perhaps, its smooth fondant icing a reminder that it's always possible to create order out of chaos; to take all of life's disappointments and cloak them in something sweet.

1. **In preparation for my date with Chris, I will not eat any of my own cake. And I might skip lunch too.**

The words make her feel so sad, she has to remind herself that this is actually a happy list; that sometimes the road to joy is about sacrifice; a painful, low-calorie odyssey through hell.

2. **I will make a conscious effort to enjoy my day at work (and not think about doing it all again tomorrow, and the day after, and the day after, ad infinitum).**

She flails for something else.

3. **I will smile whenever possible.**

To practise the mechanics involved, she smiles to herself, in that instant making eye contact with the handsome man of mystery.

He looks confused.

Then worried.

They both look away.

*

After accidentally smiling at *that* man on the train, there's something reassuring about reaching the office. As she sits down at her desk, she wonders if this is how prisoners feel: desperate to be free, and yet safely cocooned from the challenges and pitfalls of the world outside.

Geneva arrives not long after, sinking into her chair with the kind of weary sigh ill-suited to someone who travels to work by cab. She nods at Alice's cake tin. 'Let's see it, then,' she says, sounding more like a nurse at an STD clinic.

Alice carries the open tin to Geneva's desk. 'It's a Victoria sponge. But I've also put some lemon zest in there to give it a little zing.'

Geneva peers at it, seems unimpressed. 'I'm afraid I don't eat gluten on weekdays. And my nutritionist has told me I can only have organic, grass-fed dairy. From Alpine cows. I'm assuming that's not.'

'It is doubtful,' replies Alice.

She turns around to find Piers sitting on her desk. 'May I?' he says, beckoning her closer.

She carries the cake to him, feeling more and more like a door-to-door salesman. 'It's a Victoria sponge.'

'It looks lovely,' he says, giving her a smile that feels inappropriate for a mere cake. He lowers his voice. 'This all feels very domesticated, don't you think?'

'It's just a cake,' she replies. 'I make them all the time.'

Piers raises his voice, clearly wants Geneva to hear too. 'Have you ever made that cake for Ben?'

Geneva takes the bait. 'Yes, how is Ben?'

Alice glares at him before turning to Geneva and forcing a smile. 'He's very well, thank you.'

'Are you making him fatter?' she says. 'Because that's what happens, apparently. It's statistically proven. By dating someone like you, his body mass index will go through the roof. Give it a year or two and everyone will just assume that his mother was fucked by a slug.'

Alice holds up the cake. 'I should really take this to the pantry and get it ready for everyone.'

She walks away, only realizing as she gets there that Piers has followed her. 'So how's life, Alice? You know, outside the office.'

'Piers, I'm not very comfortable with that question.'

'Why? I always ask questions like that.'

'True, but after our lunch...'

'I thought we'd agreed to never discuss that again? You disappoint me.'

Her phone starts to ring. 'Excuse me,' she says, deciding that this is the perfect moment to put Piers on hold.

As she answers the call, it's Chris's voice that bounces down the line. 'Alice, it's me again. Can you talk?'

'Chris, I'm in a meeting right now.'

'I'm sorry, I've just realized I'm double-booked tomorrow night. How about Thursday instead?'

Alice glances at Piers, who's doing a bad job of pretending not to listen to her every word. 'You know what?' she tells Chris. 'I think we should do it on Saturday.' She notices Piers

195

twitch. 'We can make a big night of it. A massive night. The sky's the limit.' There's a dazed silence at the other end of the line, Chris doubtless looking like he's just struck gold. 'I have to go now, but we'll talk soon, okay?' As she hangs up, she gives Piers her sweetest smile. 'Sorry about that. Where were we?'

'Who's Chris?'

'He's… my boyfriend.' She watches his face drop. 'It's a new relationship, just in the last day or two.'

'Not the vegan, surely?'

'What can I say? We had a date and, er, one thing led to another. It's turned into something very intense. Very passionate, in fact. We're even talking about children. Though not any time soon. I really want to focus on my career for the next decade or two, at least.'

Piers takes his time to respond. 'To be frank, Alice, I imagine that Chris is no better than me: only chasing after you because he thinks you're the kind of person who'll say yes to anything.' He waits, perhaps wanting to see the hurt in her eyes as the words sink in. 'But, of course, you're a smart girl. I'm sure you're not so naïve as to think that all this attention means you're genuinely desired. Trust me when I say, Alice, that will never be the case for someone like you.'

Maidstone, Kent
34 miles from Alice

Ben knew that the funeral would be a low-key affair, but he hadn't expected it to feel so unworthy of his grandfather. It doesn't help that the chapel is empty – just Ben and his grandmother sitting in the front row – or that the minister has to refer to his notes whenever mentioning Ben's grandfather by name, the echo only seeming to accentuate the fact that he knows nothing about this man.

Ben wants to barge up there and take over, if only so that his grandfather's final moments in the flesh can be what he deserves. He would stand there and tell the room – the empty room – that his grandfather was a good and upstanding man who looked after the people he loved, even though he could never tell them that he loved them. A man who lived each day with a stoic fortitude not because of his experiences, but in spite of them.

He's still thinking of the ways he would like to celebrate his grandfather's life – a man he's only come to know since he died – but then it's all over, the deep baritone of an organ playing while a man of courage slides into the flames.

Moments later, they're being ushered to the door, the minister shaking their hands as they go, giving them the same automated smile he doubtless gives everyone; just two more faces on life's never-ending conveyor belt of loss.

*

'I just wish more people could have come,' says Ben, he and his grandmother sitting in the kitchen at home, his grandfather's urn on the table between them. 'Dave wanted to, but he had a job interview this morning.'

'It's fine,' she replies, the words uttered on a gentle sigh.

'He wanted to come. It's just he's having a baby and life is—'

'Benjamin, you don't need to worry. Your grandfather never did like crowds. I think he would have been happy to know it was a private, family occasion.'

Ben notices her look at the clock. 'You don't have to go today.'

'Yes, I do,' she says.

'But after all the stress of the funeral. If you just waited another night or two…'

'The truth is I don't like being here without him. I never was, you see.' She smiles at the thought. 'It's rather remarkable, isn't it? In all the years we lived in this house, I never once spent the night without him by my side.' She reaches out and takes Ben's hand in hers. 'I know you and Neville are here for me, but I can't stay in this house, surrounded by all these memories, if he's not here too.'

The next few hours pass in a pained silence, while she makes her final preparations to leave. By the time the taxi pulls up in the driveway, the grief feels as fresh and raw as it did last week, as though Ben's grandfather has just died all over again. In those last moments, she appears overwhelmed; perhaps only realizing now that there is never enough time in which to say farewell.

'Well, I leave you in charge of the house,' she says. 'Of selling it. Of letting it all go.' She crosses to Neville's cage. 'Goodbye, my darling Neville. Be good for Benjamin, won't you?' Neville cocks his head, appears perplexed.

'I can bring him to you sometimes,' says Ben, instantly thinking it a very bad idea.

'It's a kind offer, Benjamin, but we both know it would be impossible.' She turns back to Neville. 'There comes a time for all of us when we have to part ways. I just hadn't expected it to be so soon.' Neville lets out a muted chirp, appears as sad as she is. 'Thank you for our years together, Neville. And please know I will always think of you.' She turns for the door, blinking away tears. 'I should be off before I get too sentimental.'

Neville begins calling louder and louder as she leaves the room. It's only as Ben's putting her bags in the taxi that he realizes she's stopped in the front doorway, staring back inside while Neville's mournful cries echo through the house.

'Gran? Is everything all right?'

'I was just thinking of your parents,' she says. 'Imagining how lovely it would have been to have them here, all of us together as one big family. If only we'd lived a little differently, how very happy we might have been.'

Feltham, West London

Alice groans and pulls the duvet over her head, her snooze alarm starting to ring for the fourth time this morning. Although she tries to think of good reasons to get up, it seems so much easier to make a list of all the reasons *not* to: that Piers is fundamentally evil; that Geneva is little better; that even Harry has the ability to make Alice, a dog lover, want to kick him.

She curls up, certain that this bed, right now, is more comfortable than any bed has ever been in the history of mankind. Forget the crowded, uncomfortable journey to work; forget her badly paid job. This morning she will stay in bed and allow the day to unfold as it will.

She barely notices it when the snooze alarm starts to ring for the fifth time; it's a mere sound by now. But then she hears a dull banging on the wall, and the muffled voice of Mei shouting something in Chinese. Seconds later, Mei bursts into her room, a sleep mask pushed atop her tousled bedhead. Without a word, she snatches up the alarm clock and smashes it on the floor, kicking at the plastic shards for good measure.

Wide awake now, Alice stares at the debris.

'I'll buy you a new one,' says Mei, already leaving the room.

Maidstone, Kent

42 miles from Alice

Ben had feared this moment, waking up alone in this house for the first time in his life, neither of his grandparents here to give the endless clutter any meaning. Yet it's not sadness that greets him as he opens his eyes, not even the sound of Neville out in the living room. It's Alice, sitting on the side of his bed.

'Ben,' she says, in a gentle whisper. 'Ben.'

He rubs his eyes, still sleepy. 'I thought you'd gone back to Scotland.'

'I'm wherever you are, Ben. I'll always be wherever you are.' She gives him the same sweet smile as always, her bright yellow dress seeming to illuminate the room. 'There's lots of work to be done. There's still so much to sort through.'

'Don't remind me,' replies Ben, groaning. 'I should probably just chuck it all.'

'But then you'll never know what you might have missed.' Still smiling at him, she leaves the room, everything feeling darker and emptier in her absence.

Wanting to be with her again, Ben jumps out of bed. 'Alice?'

He gets to the living room, but there's nothing to see: just Neville staring at him in silence, the room so full of boxes it looks more like a warehouse than a family home.

Mayfair, London W1

Despite the rocky start to her day with Mei, the arrival of Wednesday afternoon at least makes the week feel like a death match that Alice might actually win. She's been waiting in the conference room for almost half an hour when Geneva finally turns up for their meeting. 'God, journalists…' is all she says, as she enters the room.

'Was it not a good lunch?' replies Alice.

'On the contrary – even though I found it a totally hideous experience, I must say it went very well indeed. He loved the wine, of course, and he loved the needlessly molecular cuisine. He was almost eating it out of my hand by the time we were finished.' She fixes Alice with one of her trademark stares: the kind of look that could presage anything from an important announcement to a cold-blooded killing. 'So, what are you waiting for? Show me what you've got for the media pack.' As Alice lays out page after page, Geneva drums her fingernails on the table, looking more bored by the second. 'Okay,' she says, before Alice has even finished. 'Talk me through it.'

'There is more.'

'Don't worry, I'll just use my imagination for the rest.'

'Well, we have all the usual product shots, a description of the full product range, and I've come up with three different versions of the press release.' Geneva appears bored. 'I've also made up some cute little lists. There's a "Ten fun facts", and some product-specific stuff too, like "Ten things to do with the purple chilli sauce".' She sees Geneva grimace. 'I was thinking of edible artwork. The colours are perfect for—'

'It's fine, you don't need to say anything else. It all sounds likeyourtrademarkroutineoflet's-go-skipping-through-flower-meadows-and-hug-a-tree.'

'Is that a bad thing?' says Alice, worried.

'The real issue is, how are things between you and Ben?'

'Does that matter?'

'Inasmuch as it impacts your happiness, and your happiness impacts your ability to do your job, I'd say it's a very pertinent question.'

'Am I not doing my job very well?'

'Alice, one never takes a defensive tone in PR.'

'Okay. Ben is fine, thank you. We're both fine.'

'For Christ's sake, Alice, at least try and sell the relationship to me. If you can't make your own boyfriend sound interesting, I'm not sure how you're going to cope with a lifetime of clients like these.' She glances down at Alice's papers again. 'Give me the... how did you put it? The ten fun facts about Ben.'

'Ten is quite a lot,' says Alice.

'Then let's say five. Surprise me.'

'Well, he, um...'

'For God's sake, Alice. Just pick something.' She snaps her fingers.

'He knows how to walk a trapeze.'

'Really?' Geneva looks impressed. 'Where did he learn that?'

'Well, that's fun fact number two,' says Alice, suddenly feeling like she's on a roll; that she could, in fact, stand there all afternoon and make up endless facts about a man she doesn't know. 'Ben's grandfather was a circus performer. Of some renown.'

'Does he have gypsy blood?'

'Fun fact number three: his father was a French émigré, and his mother was, er, a Sephardic Jew.' She instantly wishes she hadn't said it. 'Maybe that even counts as three and four.'

'No, it doesn't.'

'Okay, well, four... he makes an excellent eggs benedict.'

'It sounds very domesticated, but it's hardly kosher, is it? I doubt his mother would approve. And the fact that he's already making *breakfast* for you tells me a lot more about your private life than I wanted to know. Don't tell me, fun fact number five is that he's got a fetish for body fat.'

'No, he thinks you don't pay me enough.'

There's a moment of silence. 'I'd hardly call that a *fun* fact.'

'But it's true, the salary is barely enough to get by.'

'Of course it isn't. It's not even intended to be anything as vulgar as a "salary". Before you arrived, we didn't pay our interns anything; I would have thought that this is a moment for gratitude rather than complaint.'

'But if you don't pay a living wage, then you're not going to have people like me as interns.'

'Your point being?' replies Geneva, with a laugh. Clearly tired of the conversation, she stands up. 'Alice, you'd be infinitely happier here, and fit in a good deal better, if you just thought of the remuneration as, I don't know, a little pin money to buy some new shoes once in a while.' She glances down at Alice's feet. 'Lord knows you need to.'

Maidstone, Kent
34 miles from Alice

With the house to himself, Ben has entered a new phase in the sorting process. Whereas the early days were more akin to an archaeological dig, now he tears through boxes with wild abandon. Never mind that he's creating an even bigger mess, there's only him and Neville to see it.

'You can join me if you like,' he calls, in the hope of summoning Alice, but the only response is a judgemental look from Neville. 'Or not,' he says to himself. 'I'm quite happy to work alone.'

By late afternoon, he's crawling through the dark recesses of the loft, confident that this is the final frontier; that by the time he's dragged these boxes into the daylight and sifted through their contents, this house will have no more secrets. Dragging the last of them to the open hatch, he upends them one by one, sending their contents crashing down into the hallway below; a dusty explosion of yellowing documents that probably weren't very important even when they were stuffed away decades ago: old newspapers, brittle with age; faded postcards, the senders probably long since dead.

As he empties yet another box, there's a solid *thud* on the floor below. Ben peers down, but whatever it was has already been buried in ancient knitting magazines and crumpled tobacco wrappers.

Curious now, he climbs down and begins picking through the pile until he uncovers a small leather satchel, its corners scuffed to the texture of sandpaper. He picks it up and peers inside, but there's nothing to see. After days and days of sorting through things just like this – junk that his grandparents had ferreted away for years – Ben tosses it back on the heap, is climbing up into the loft again when he stops and decides to take a closer look.

He carries it into the daylight of the living room, Neville greeting him with a slight chirp, though showing no interest in any further contact.

'This could have been mine,' says Ben, still inspecting the satchel. 'It looks like a kid's bag, don't you think?'

He slings it over his shoulder and strikes a pose, but Neville's only reaction is to close his eyes. Taking it to the window, Ben stretches back the flap and peers inside again, the sunlight revealing the dark brown colour of the torn cotton lining. And there, on the inside flap, one simple word scratched into the leather in the unsteady hand of a young child: 'Ben'.

'Bloody hell,' he says, staring at this scuffed little satchel like it's a priceless treasure. 'It *was* mine, it really was.' He looks even more closely at his name, the writing suggestive of a child who's only just learnt the alphabet; who's only just realized the alchemy of adding letters to letters to conjure oneself. 'I must have been young,' he says, 'very young.' He glances at Neville, hopeful that he may want to share in this epochal moment, but still he just sits there, eyes shut to the world. Putting the bag back over his shoulder, Ben goes out to the hallway, looks at himself in the mirror while he tries to recall how it felt to wear this bag all those years ago.

He sticks his hand inside, pretends to rummage around and pull something out. 'Lemon bonbons,' he says, not even aware of the words until he sees his reflection, standing there offering him an invisible bag of sweets. 'Always lemon,' he says, sadder now but unsure why.

As he pretends to put the sweets away, he feels something behind the ripped inner lining. Taking the bag off, he pushes his fingers in, probing deep inside. And there it is again, between his fingertips now: something stiff and glossy. He pulls at it, but it only gets snared in the frayed cotton. Turning on the hallway light, he peers closer, this time seeing the corner of a Polaroid poking out from the torn fabric.

As he gently tugs at it and more of the picture comes into view, he realizes what it is; understands that this picture is far more important than the bag will ever be. Ripping the fabric now, he pulls the photo free, the bag falling to the floor as he stares at what's in his hands. There he is as a young boy, sitting on a small bicycle, stabilizers on the rear wheel. And beside him, also on a bicycle, a young woman in a yellow dress, glowing in the bright Indian sunshine. At first glance she looks just like Alice, but even as Ben's eyes begin to fill with tears, he already knows the difference: this woman's smile feels like home.

Feltham, West London

Mei kept her promise to buy a new alarm clock, but Alice doesn't get the chance to try it. Instead, she's woken up shortly after six o'clock in the morning by the sound of Mei on the phone to her parents in Shanghai. Lying there in bed, bleary-eyed and half-awake, Alice wonders if Mei's family conversations always sound this way, like screamed threats of blackmail and parricide. Given the tone of what's being said, Alice assumes that they're talking about money; Mei not biting the hand that feeds her so much as going straight for the jugular. She raises her voice further, shouting so loudly now that she possibly wouldn't need a phone in order to be heard in China.

Much like a horror film, it culminates in a scream, and then an eerie silence. Alice waits in bed; has seen enough movies to know that this can't be the end: any second now, Mei will surely start screaming again, possibly even burst into the room with an axe. And yet the minutes tick by; not a sound.

Finally, Alice gets up, opens her bedroom door with a well-practised stealth.

No sign of Mei.

Wearing her fluffy Justin Bieber slippers, she shuffles down the hallway. Just as she reaches the bathroom, Mei appears from nowhere. 'I didn't know you were up,' she says.

Alice, who presumes the whole street is up by now, simply continues into the bathroom. As she locks the door behind

211

her, she can hear Mei pressing herself up against it. 'I'm putting your rent up, effective immediately.'

Alice opens the door. 'Mei, you can't just—'

'It's my flat.'

'Yes, but we have a *contract*. There are laws.' She notices Mei hesitate, perhaps considering whether this is a law she can get away with breaking. It's the same look that Alice can imagine on her face throughout the day: *Should I pay for these shoes or steal them? Shall I just shout at this person or kill them?*

'Okay,' says Mei. 'But you owe me money for the new clock. You need to pay me because I bought it.'

'Only because you broke my old one.'

'I didn't break it. It… it slipped from my hands.' Alice starts to close the door, Mei shouting through the narrowing gap. 'Just give me fifty pounds and we'll forget it.'

Again, Alice stops, the door still ajar. 'Mei, that clock is a lump of mass-produced plastic. It's the single-cell organism of clocks.' She sees the confusion on Mei's face. 'There's no way it cost fifty pounds.'

'But you're forgetting about my time. My time is very valuable.' Alice shuts the door in her face. 'I could charge you double and it would still be cheap.' In the silence that follows, Alice assumes that Mei has gone, but then her voice comes shouting through the door again. 'Remember to flush the toilet this time, you animal.'

Alice snatches the door open. 'Mei, what are you talking about? I always flush.'

'Ancient Chinese proverb: "Big meaty poo cannot come from small dog."'

'Really?' says Alice. 'That's a Chinese proverb?'

'Of course not! See, you're racist too. You think everyone in my country is stupid.' She storms towards her room, shouting as she goes. 'Maybe you can fool other people with that "sweet little fat girl" routine, but not me, Alice. I know you're a monster.'

As soon as Alice leaves the flat, it's clear what she needs to do. While she walks to the train station, she starts practising what she will say to her father, the chill morning air transforming her muttered words into faint wisps of vapour. *Interest rates are low; it makes sense to buy a place now. Could you please help me with the deposit?*

By the time the station is in sight, she's said it to herself so many times that it feels natural and right – so natural that she stops and makes the call there on the street in Feltham, the distant sound of Heathrow a reminder that there's a whole world waiting to be discovered.

Her father answers on the third ring. 'Alice, it's not like you to call this early. Is everything all right?'

'I'm fine,' she replies, all sense of certainty draining away. 'I just, er, wanted to hear your voice, that's all.'

'How lovely. Are you at work already?'

'On my way,' she says, aware that even this isn't true; she's standing still, going nowhere. 'It was lovely to see you the other day, but I never got a chance to talk to you about that exhibition you went to.'

'Oh, *that*. Let's just say it was enlightening, in very unexpected ways.'

'See, that sounds interesting. I wish we could spend more time together, just you and me.'

'You know, I've been thinking exactly the same thing.'

'Really?' she says, her mood instantly lifting; the words she wants to say seeming within reach again. *Please help me buy a flat of my own. Please help me feel like my adult life is beginning.*

'I think we should sit down, just you and me, and have a good chat.'

'I'd love that.'

'Quite a lot has happened in the last few days and you need to know about it.'

'Is everything all right?' she says, her confidence in retreat now.

'Yes, yes. It's just your mother and I have decided to make some important changes in our lives. Changes that will affect you.'

'Are you divorcing?'

'Of course not,' he replies, his tone of incredulity at total odds with everything he's said for the last five years. 'We've merely come to the conclusion that our lives should be lived differently. It's nothing to concern yourself about.' A brief pause. 'Though I do think we need to discuss things sooner rather than later.'

'See, when you say it like that, I feel *more* worried, not less.'

'I'll come up to town next week. Let's have dinner on Monday night. Just the two of us.'

Maidstone, Kent
34 miles from Alice

Dave and Agnes arrive in a flurry of domesticated chaos, the two of them already looking like a married couple. Although Agnes's bump isn't showing yet, Ben can see the change in her; a rounding of edges, both literal and otherwise.

'Look at you,' he says, trying not to say the words in his mouth. *You're about to inflate. In another month or two, you'll look like a balloon animal.*

She pulls him into an embrace, unexpectedly tender. 'How are you coping?' she says.

'It's definitely been a week of discoveries.'

'Dave and I have been talking about the baby. We want you to be a godfather.'

'Me?' says Ben, shocked. 'You mean it?'

'Just remember that's godfather with a small g, not a capital.

214

We don't want you getting all Don Corleone on us.' She wanders over to the birdcage, where Neville sits pressed against the bars, peering out with all the doe-eyed innocence of Orphan Annie. 'He's cute,' she says.

'Trust me, looks can be deceiving.' He sees her put a finger inside the cage. 'Don't!' he yells, but Neville just sits there while she rubs the back of his head.

'I don't think you should be taking this parrot home if you don't know how to look after him.'

'That's easy for you to say, you don't know him,' says Ben. 'He's manipulating you. Anyway, what am I supposed to do with him? That kind of parrot can live to seventy. He's basically going to outlive us all. It's like he's immortal or something.' By now Neville is leaning into Agnes's touch, his eyes closed. 'I don't think he's going to like living in London much. I doubt the neighbours will be thrilled with it either. Part of me wonders if I shouldn't just move in here.'

'Are you mad?' says Agnes.

'I could settle down, couldn't I?'

'Settle down and do what?'

'I don't know. Have a go at the kind of life my grandparents had. They were happy.'

'Ben, ignoring the fact that you're only twenty-three, if you move in here, it'll just be you lost in someone else's life. The whole point of adulthood is to go and live your own.' She glances out the window, appears confused. 'Why is there a piano in the garden?'

'I'll show you later,' replies Ben. 'Right now, how about I make us all a cup of tea?'

She instantly stops massaging Neville. 'I'll make it myself, thank you very much. Even at your ripe age, you have no clue how to make a decent cuppa.' She wanders from the room, clearly unsure where to find the kitchen.

Alone now, Ben turns to Dave, lowers his voice. 'I did that

215

on purpose. There's something I need to show you.' He urges Dave towards the hallway. After pausing briefly to make sure that Agnes is out of sight, he hurries to his bedroom, closes the door behind them. 'I've found a picture of my mother.'

'Ben, that's amazing. I'm so happy for you.' He begins to look confused. 'So what's the problem?'

Even in there, just the two of them, Ben replies in a whisper. 'She's just like Alice. The spitting image, in fact.' He waits for Dave to look repulsed, but still there's nothing. 'Don't you get it? It's creepy. It's Oedipal.'

'That's a very big word for you.'

'I learnt it last night, while I was Googling weird, fucked-up people who develop a sexual attraction to their mothers.' He passes the photo to Dave. 'Here…'

'Oh, mate, that's beautiful.'

'It is, isn't it?' He smiles at the sight of it. 'But I don't know, it's an odd feeling. The Alice thing has spoilt it a bit. It's like I've taken the one thing I've always wanted, and ruined it.'

'You weren't to know.'

'Tell that to my subconscious.'

'Ben, you were only young when you last saw her.'

The words distract him. 'I reckon I must be about four or five in that picture.' He leans closer to get a better look. 'It might have been taken just weeks, maybe even days, before the accident.'

Saying nothing, Dave simply puts his arm around Ben, the two of them staring at it together; at Ben and his mother all those years ago, both of them smiling for the camera, blissfully unaware of what the future would bring.

★

Agnes sleeps in the spare room while Ben and Dave pack the rented van with all the things that he's taking back to London.

'Is she ever going to wake up?' says Ben, he and Dave long since finished. 'It's been hours already.'

'Yeah, she's been doing this a lot recently.'

'And it's only going to get worse, isn't it? In a few months' time, it'll be like a waking nightmare; this woman you don't even recognize anymore. And that's just the prelude to years of hell.'

'Thanks, Ben. I appreciate that.'

Ben, Dave and Neville return to sitting in silence; three men with a lot on their minds. It's Agnes who brings things back to life, stumbling into the room, looking groggy. 'Why didn't someone wake me up sooner?'

'Because we value our lives,' says Dave.

'But it's getting late.'

'We've already finished packing the van,' says Ben. He glances at Neville's cage. 'Except for you know who, of course.'

She goes to him. 'Do you think he'll be okay on the drive into town?'

'Don't know, don't care,' replies Ben, getting up. 'But now that you're awake, I can show you why there's a piano in the garden.'

'As long as you're not going to play it. I don't think I'm ready for music right now.'

'Trust me,' says Ben, fetching a bottle of lighter fluid, 'I'm definitely not going to play it.'

He goes out to the garden, starts to douse the piano.

Agnes sounds alarmed. 'Ben, you can't do that.'

'My grandmother doesn't want it.'

'But someone might.'

'It hasn't been touched in over twenty years. It probably doesn't even work anymore.'

'Still, it's a *piano*. It just seems wrong.'

'If you knew its history, you'd realize we should have done this years ago.'

He doesn't stop until the bottle is empty, the air thick with the smell of petroleum. By now, Dave and Agnes look too shocked to speak.

'All right,' says Ben. 'Are we ready?'

'Not really,' replies Dave.

Ben strikes a match and tosses it, the fire spreading in an instant. He stands back as a wave of heat surges towards him, the fire already taking hold. Within thirty seconds the wood is beginning to crack and splinter, and soon the strings inside are snapping in explosive, off-key snatches of sound.

'See,' he says, 'it's horribly out of tune.'

And although Agnes still looks appalled by the spectacle, Ben can imagine that if his grandparents were there, they would be dancing around the fire by now, shrieking and laughing in the flickering light, both of them finally set free from the past.

Brixton, London SW2

13 miles from Alice

Neville likes Ben's flat as much as Ben likes having him there. He bursts into life this morning at the same time that Ben's grandparents would have been getting up, two old people padding about in the pre-dawn hours. While Ben lies in bed and tries to pretend that it's not happening, Neville squawks and screams, occasionally banging his beak against the bars of his cage for added emphasis. At length, when Ben – and presumably the neighbours too – can take it no more, he drags himself to the living room, which Neville's giant cage has transformed from an awkward, badly furnished room into a cramped and totally unliveable space.

'What?' shouts Ben. Neville glowers at him, his bulging eyes and cocked head appearing even more aggressive than normal. 'Remember this: you'd probably taste like chicken.'

Neville dives for his seed bowl, starts throwing liberal scatterings onto the sofa and across the floor. By now Dave is also awake, standing in his bedroom doorway, a baggy pair of Y-fronts ballooning around him. To his credit he seems to take it all in his stride; possibly views the noise and chaos as valuable training for the long years of parenthood that lie ahead.

'Where did I put his blanket?' says Ben.

Dave points to it in the corner of the room, watches as Ben hurries to pick it up.

'This is why I don't feel sorry for you,' says Ben, shouting to him over the sound of Neville's screams. 'In about eighteen years, your kid is going to piss off to university and leave you in peace. Whereas I'll have Neville until the day I die.' Neville screams even louder at the mention of his name. 'Or until something happens that tragically cuts short his life.'

As he tosses the blanket over Neville's cage, he can feel the sunflower seeds wedged between his toes, already knows that he'll be finding them down the side of the sofa for months to come.

'I'll say this,' says Dave, 'he's a very effective alarm clock.'

'Yeah, if I needed to wake up at five in the morning, I'd be thrilled.'

'Well,' says Dave, yawning, 'I'm going back to sleep.'

'Sorry about all this. For Neville. For everything.'

'It's okay,' replies Dave. 'I wanted to be here on your first night back.' His eyes shift to the floor. 'Though I'll be staying at Agnes's place tonight. There's a bunch of stuff she wants me to do over there, so I'll probably head off this morning, right after breakfast.'

'Okay,' says Ben, trying not to look dejected.

'It's nothing to do with Neville.'

'No, of course, you've got responsibilities, haven't you? You're all grown up.' He tries to say it with a smile, but the words have a mournful ring to them. Standing there, Dave isn't just on the other side of the room, it feels like he's on the opposite shore of some ever-widening gulf; physically the same pudgy Dave that Ben remembers from their years together, but becoming a real grown-up now; a wise and sensible man; a dad.

Soho, London W1

After a long and busy day at work, this should be a relaxed dinner, Alice and Rachel meeting for a cheap pizza just as

222

they have done on many other Fridays, but tonight Rachel is too distracted by the thought of starting her new job, her mood casting a dark shadow over the evening.

'You might love the job,' says Alice, certain that this isn't true, but thinking it the right thing to say. 'And remember, it's the start of financial independence.'

'Is that true in a city like London? They could pay me double and it still wouldn't be enough to afford anything more than a crap room in a shit part of town.'

'It *is* your first job. You have to start somewhere.'

'Is that what you tell yourself every day?'

This dampens the mood even more. 'At least the pizza's good,' says Alice, trying to fill the silence. She reaches for another slice, but stops. 'No, I've probably had too much already. I should think of the calories. I should think of what the slim-trim-Alice would want me to do.'

Rachel grabs the slice, tosses it on to Alice's plate. 'Is Ben that judgemental? I don't think you should spend your time with someone who makes you feel bad.'

'There is no Ben.' For a second, she wishes she could just leave it there; liberated by a moment of undiluted truth. 'What I mean is, we've stopped seeing each other.'

Rachel appears heartened by the news, her mood subtly improving. 'When did that happen?'

'Er, recently. What matters is that I know in my heart it's the right thing to do; to let him go and move on with my life.' She smiles to herself, feeling free for the first time in weeks. 'As nice as it was to meet Ben — and it was nice, it really was — I want it known that there is officially no Ben in my life, and frankly I'm looking forward to telling the whole world that.'

Rachel has the approximation of a smile now, the evening beginning to seem more upbeat and hopeful. 'I want you to remember,' she says, 'even if you never find another man, you will always have me.'

'Well, believe it or not, I have a date tomorrow. Someone I met at a party.'

'When were you at a party?' says Rachel, managing to sound both confused and hurt.

'It was Frida, from the homeless feeding. I wanted to invite you, but she can be difficult, you know how it is…' Despite being untrue, the words seem to help. 'And you didn't miss much. It was a roomful of vegans.'

'So your date tomorrow night is with a guy who eats no animal products?'

'I know! And here's me; I'd buy bacon toothpaste if I could.'

'You do realize the whole date's going to be a total disaster?'

Alice finds the words unexpectedly hurtful, but they seem to energize Rachel, and now Alice can think only of sustaining the momentum. 'It's definitely not my idea of romance, the two of us sitting down to a candlelit dinner of nut cutlets.'

'So why even bother going?'

'Well, he's a nice guy.'

'Ben was a nice guy, but it didn't last.'

'True, but without going into excessive detail, there are significant differences between Ben and Chris.'

'And let's not forget, you said your boss was a nice guy too.'

Alice's mind returns to what Piers said on Tuesday: that no man will ever genuinely want someone like her. 'It can be so hard to know what a man's thinking…'

'The way I see it, your biggest problem is that you attract manipulative people into your life.' Rachel starts on another slice of pizza. 'For your sake, I'm just relieved that you've got me too.'

Soho, London W1
300 yards from Alice

With Dave away until tomorrow, Ben finds himself drifting through the streets of London, reluctant to go home. It was fun at first, doing all the things that tourists do: listening to the buskers in Covent Garden; wandering across to Piccadilly Circus and up through the backstreets of Soho, the bars buzzing with Friday night revellers. After all the drama and upheaval of recent days, it feels as if he needs this process of re-acquaintance; as though he's been away from London for so much longer than just two weeks. But as it gets later and later, being outside stops being fun. A chill wind is telling Ben to go home, but still he lingers in Soho – looking at restaurants that he can't afford, taking detours that hold no appeal – all to delay the moment when he returns home to Neville and an empty flat.

It's the rain that finally drives him back there. He gets home to find the place is dark, silent and fragrance-free, a reminder that everything in his life has changed. The sight of Neville doesn't help. There are no squawks and cries this evening, just a parrot sitting in gloomy silence, the floor of the cage now littered with feathers.

'Please tell me this is normal,' says Ben. 'Please tell me that this is just some moulting thing.'

Neville moves to the corner of the cage, sits with his back to Ben. The peace and quiet should feel good, but seeing Neville hunkered down like this only makes Ben feel like he's party to some great injustice; that he's somehow holding this animal against its will, slowly destroying its sanity in the same way that Neville is slowly destroying his. And as Ben stands there, watching his nemesis ignore him, all he can think is that Dave will soon move out for ever, and then he will be left alone with this bird, the two of them wanting nothing except their old lives back.

Brixton, London SW2

13 miles from Alice

When Ben first opens the door to Agnes, he stays there holding it open for Dave too.

'He's not coming,' she says. 'He's manning the stall.'

'You left him alone at the market?'

'He'll be fine on his own, he just doesn't know it yet. Let's face it, if he can't handle a few friendly customers, he's not going to get far with a kid, is he?'

'Are you ready for it to be a teenager?'

'Ben, I'm only just getting my head around it being a baby. I think I'd rather take it one step at a time.' She crosses to Neville's cage. 'I hear you're having a hard time with him.'

'He's started pulling his feathers out. According to some websites I checked, it's grief. The way I feel right now, I could pull my hair out too.'

Neville immediately responds to Agnes's presence. With a muted chirp, he moves closer to her.

'Do you think he's going to be okay?' she says.

'I don't know. I've spent years wishing him dead, and now I'm terrified he's dying.'

'Everything's changed so quickly, the two of you probably just need some time to adapt.' She starts to rub Neville's neck. 'If it's any consolation, we're feeling a bit overwhelmed too. I can't even remember the people we used to be just a few weeks ago.'

'I know all about that feeling.'

'And it's okay, Ben. Struggling with it doesn't make you a bad person.' Still being rubbed, Neville closes his eyes, appears content at last. 'Have you thought of finding Neville a new home? Maybe with someone who actually likes parrots?'

'I can't do that. It's the only thing I've got left from my grandparents.'

'He's a living thing, not an heirloom. Maybe the nicest way to celebrate your grandparents' life – and to make sense of your own, for that matter – is to find Neville a happy home.'

'Yeah, well, it's not that simple.' He avoids looking at her as he says it; knows that it's a lie. 'Let's not forget, Neville will be all I have for company once Dave's moved out.'

'I'm taking away your best friend, aren't I?'

'No, we're all mates. I'm… happy for you.' It's only as he says the words that he realizes how much effort they require. 'I suppose me and Dave had to grow up sooner or later. I'd just always hoped it'd be me first.'

*

Agnes has barely left the flat when Ben picks up the phone and calls Dave. After the inevitable ringing – doubtless while Dave puts down whatever he's eating – his voice calls back. 'Ben, mate.'

'Do you think the bike's still there?'

'Good morning to you too.'

'Come on, Dave, I'm serious. Do you think it's still up there?'

'At the bottom of a river, you mean? Yes, I would imagine so.'

'And how would you rate our chances if we wanted to, I don't know, fish it out?'

'Ben, I'm not going scuba diving in the Fens trying to find a bike. Anyway, I thought Glasgow was off the agenda?'

'It is. I'm very happy to say that I'm not seeing Alice anymore. By which I mean, I won't be seeing Alice again.'

'Thank you, Ben. I do understand the English language.'

'I was just thinking I could go and cycle around the Peak District for a while, as a sort of tribute to my granddad. And I could even keep riding north, couldn't I? I could aim for John O'Groats or something. If I'm lucky, I might even raise some money for those orphans after all. Though there is something I need to ask you first.'

'Okay...' replies Dave, sounding worried now.

'Do you promise not to forget me once you're a family man?'

'What sort of question is that?'

'It's just, it's like you're climbing the ladder of adulthood without me. I know it sounds mad, but it feels like I'm being left behind.'

'Ben, we're best mates. Nothing's going to change that. And as for being a dad...' He pauses, the word clearly still possessing the power to leave him speechless. 'Trust me, once that happens, I'm going to need you more than ever.'

Hoxton, London N1

It's possible that Alice has chosen the wrong venue. It was obvious that she couldn't meet Chris somewhere quiet – she didn't want other people listening to them as they navigate their first real date – but now she suspects that she may have gone a little too far in the other direction: there's such a seething mass of people pressing up against the bar, it's feasible that they will soon spill over the top, the whole room slowly beginning to fill with bodies.

She sits astride two stools at the bar, determined to protect her slice of precious real estate despite being jostled on all sides by lithe young women in plaid shirts, and bearded men with tattoo sleeves, everyone doubtless having got there on fixed-gear bicycles. As she dodges someone's elbow, an older man speaks to her, raising his voice over the din of the crowd.

'Let me buy you a drink.'

'No, thanks, I'm—'

'Come on, I won't take no for an answer. Have a G&T.' Before she can say anything, he's flagged down a bartender and ordered their drinks. He turns back to her, leaning in so close that she can smell the cologne on his skin, the scent of a man expecting to score. 'The name's Mike.'

Alice braces herself to shoo him away. 'Look, I'm here to meet—'

'I had to have my dog put down yesterday. He was old and in pain, so it was the right thing to do, but still…' He gives her a wistful smile. 'It's good to have some company.'

All the words she wants to say are still in her mouth – *I'm here to meet a guy I like, not babysit a stranger* – but, as ever, she can't say them; her own needs overridden once again by the feeling that she must always accommodate other people's demands and desires.

As the bartender brings their drinks, she notices Chris on the far side of the room, slowly edging his way towards them.

Mike raises his glass. 'Here's to a great night.' Frustrated now, Alice snatches hers up and downs it in one. 'Wow,' he says, staring at her empty glass, 'you're thirsty.'

He tries to flag down the bartender again – all the while Chris getting closer and closer.

'I'm a lesbian,' shouts Alice. This finally gets his attention. 'Sorry, I should have mentioned it before, but I've, er, only just come out of the closet. It's been a difficult process.' She notices a new look on his face now: the mental arithmetic of a man wondering whether she'll go home with him for old time's sake. 'I'm here to meet a gay friend of mine. I think the two of you would get on really, really well. You're definitely his type.' She points at Chris, not far off. 'Look, he's just coming.'

Mike starts backing away. 'No, no, the two of you probably want to chat. I respect that.'

'Thanks for the drink,' she says, but he's already vanishing into the crowd.

Chris reaches her side, the throng pressing his body against hers. 'Sorry,' he says, 'it's packed in here.' He notices her empty glass. 'Have you been waiting long?'

'Not really.'

'But long enough, obviously.'

'It was nice,' she says, already feeling a little tipsy. 'I wouldn't mind another.'

'Well, Alice,' he replies, with a laugh, 'I do believe you're out to have a good time.'

'No, no, I'm not Alice,' she says, suddenly struck by the thought that if she's not herself, then maybe Chris too will not be like everyone else in her life. 'My name's Chloë. And until recently I was a nun. Living in a convent.'

'Then it sounds to me,' he replies, eyes sparkling, 'you need someone to teach you about the ways of the world.'

*

The rest of the evening is a blur. Although Alice is fairly sure they left the bar quite early, they were there long enough to start kissing. After one especially passionate embrace, she recalls catching sight of Mike, still alone, watching them from the far side of the room. She tried to wave goodbye as they left, but he simply looked away, evidently too confused by the complexities of human sexuality.

Amid her fractured memories of the night, Alice remembers going for burgers – though where they went or how they got there is a mystery. All she can picture is Chris eating a tofu burger with vegan cheese, whereas she was sitting there with the real deal, pink meaty juices dripping through her fingers while she explained that the nuns never allowed them to eat their meat bloody; never allowed them to touch anything as phallic as French fries.

It's difficult to say how the rest of the evening went. All

she knows is that she's now walking with Chris through darkened streets, the cold night air making it easier to think.

'We'd both feel much better lying down,' he says, making a brazen invitation to sex sound strangely gallant.

'You can't just say that to a nun,' replies Alice. 'Woo me.'

'Come on, Ali—'

'No, no. Just a bit longer.' She can hear a faint slur in her words, the voice seeming to come from elsewhere. 'This is fun, don't you think? To forget who we are. To just… forget.'

Chris rallies. 'Well, it's true I've had a wonderful evening. I've enjoyed your company tremendously, and I think the nuns' loss is my gain.' He appears to stoop a little, too tired to resist gravity. 'And now, to complete the evening, I would like to take you home and introduce you to the joys of sex.'

He flags down a passing taxi and gently shepherds her into it, drunkenly clambering in after her.

They've only driven for a minute or two when Alice sees a clothes donation bank on the side of the road. 'Stop!' she yells to the driver.

'What's happening?' says Chris, as the car pulls to an abrupt halt.

'Prove to me how much you want to take me home.' Seeing his confusion, she points at the donation bank. 'A charitable man is a sexy man.'

Grinning now, he scrambles from the car. Staggering towards the donation bank, he pulls off his shirt, drops it in. He turns to face Alice, arms open as if expecting applause.

Alice shakes her head. 'I think you can afford to be a little more generous than that.'

Still smiling, he kicks off his shoes and socks, throws them in too. Under her watchful gaze, he starts undoing his belt and loosening his trousers.

'Come on,' she says. 'You're doing well.'

He hands her his wallet and keys, then clumsily steps out of his trousers and throws them in, before tiptoeing back towards the car in nothing but his boxers.

Alice leans from the window. 'No, no,' she slurs. 'Think of the needy people out there who could make good use of your underwear.'

Perhaps sensing that the end is in sight, and aware of the sizeable rewards that await, he runs back to the donation bank. With a deft move, his shorts are off and into the container.

While he's still revelling in his new-found freedom, Alice shouts to the driver. 'You can go now.'

'You what?' he replies.

'Go, go!'

Chris runs after them, but it's too late. Alice leans from the window again, calling to him as the cab accelerates down the street. 'When you get to my place, I'm all yours.'

Feltham, West London

Alice wakes up to find herself spread-eagled on her bed, every limb seeming to point in a different direction, as if she fell there from a great height. She rolls onto her side and curls up, wanting only to stay like that for the rest of the day. But then she notices Chris's wallet and keys on her bedside table.

'Oh, God,' she says, with a groan, the memories of last night beginning to come screaming through the fog. Forcing herself to get up, she staggers out to the living room, hopeful that Chris will be sleeping on the sofa, looking as bad as she feels. Her head pounding, she finds the living room pristine and empty, the silence of the flat beginning to feel ominous now.

She stumbles back into her room and looks under the bed, but there's no sign of him. In her desperation, she even considers knocking on Mei's door, but it's hard to imagine that Mei, a person who seemingly hates all living things, is now harbouring a naked stranger.

Trying to stay calm, she calls his mobile phone, is encouraged when she hears ringing at the other end of the line, but seconds later there's a muffled sound from beneath her crumpled bedclothes.

'Oh, God, I took his phone too,' she says. 'I took his phone, his wallet and his keys. And left him alone in the middle of London. Naked.'

*

A few minutes later, she's staring at her telephone, frightened of calling Chris's flat, but commanding her fingers to do it anyway. As it starts to ring, she quietly hopes that it will go through to voicemail; that she can leave an apologetic message, without having to engage in a post-mortem of the evening.

But then it's Chris, his voice sounding small and sleep-fuddled. 'Hello?'

Alice takes a moment to summon the right tone. 'Chris, I'm so sorry.'

'You.'

'How did you—'

'Do you still have my phone and my wallet?'

'And your keys.'

'Which are pretty useless after I needed to get a locksmith in here at four in the morning.'

'You could have come here.'

'Yes, and killed you with my bare hands.'

'Please—'

'All I want you to do is drop my wallet and phone back here.'

'Shall I bring you something to eat too? Some tofu—'

'Alice, just put them in my mailbox. I don't want to see you or talk to you, or hear that you're sorry. I've had a long, long night. I just want to sleep.'

'Oh, all ri—' replies Alice, but he's already hung up.

Maidstone, Kent
38 miles from Alice

The nursing home feels like a members-only club, that's the way it seems to Ben this morning; a place reserved for people who've successfully navigated the twists and turns of everyday

240

life, who've made it all the way to old age – no mean feat when even a single day can be such a struggle.

He finds his grandmother poring over a jigsaw puzzle, spending more time admiring the picture on the lid than sorting through the pieces themselves, as though the box is an oversize postcard and the puzzle pieces are simply part of the packaging.

She holds the picture up as Ben approaches: a moated castle, all ivy and ancient stone.

'Isn't it pretty?' she says. 'I'd love to see it one day.'

'I can take you there if you want,' says Ben, certain that he can make *that* happen even if so many other tasks in life are beyond his abilities right now. 'How are you, Gran?'

'Everything's lovely,' she replies. 'Though I do miss my Neville. How is he?'

'Yeah, I think he misses you too...' The words bring to mind the sight of him as Ben left the flat a couple of hours earlier: huddled in the corner of his cage, big bald patches where a loud and boisterous personality used to be. 'I'm not sure he should be living with me. I don't think he's happy with me.'

'That's because he hates you, darling, he always has. I'd just imagined, with everything that's happened, the two of you would have kissed and made up by now.' She sounds disappointed, though whether it's with Ben or Neville, it's impossible to tell.

'I was thinking, maybe I could find him a new home, the right home. With someone who loves parrots, who maybe even has others, so Neville will have some company too.'

She looks around the room, a smile on her face. 'It is nice to have other people to talk to.'

'I've also decided to start my bike ride again, to ride through the Peak District.'

'That was all about a girl, wasn't it?'

'Well, originally, but—'

'There's no need for buts, Benjamin. It's the twenty-first century. You're finally free to enjoy the love that once dare not speak its name. What a wondrous time we live in.'

'I just want to finish the ride for Granddad's sake.'

'You should take him with you. The urn's right there. He always wanted to visit the Peak District.'

'But he should stay with you.'

'Please, I already have him in here,' she says, putting a hand on her heart. 'And it would be good for the two of you to spend some time together, don't you think?'

Ben hesitates. 'There's something else I wanted to show you. I found it up in the loft.' He takes the picture from his bag, hands it to her with a reverence that will forever feel appropriate.

'Oh, my,' she says, with a gasp. 'Oh, my, my, my.' She stares at it for the longest time, wiping away a tear as she looks back at him. 'You were right, Benjamin. She does have eyes just like yours.'

Acton, London W3

Today of all days, this is not where Alice should be, not what she should be doing. She arrives at the homeless feeding so late, Frida has almost finished the preparations, and there's already a queue of people outside.

'I'd given up hope of seeing you this morning,' she says, as Alice hurriedly pulls on an apron.

'I'm so sorry, it's been a—'

'No, no, it's fine,' replies Frida, with a warmth that seems out of character. 'After your big date last night, I just assumed that you and Chris were, how shall I say? Loved up.'

Thankfully, she opens the door at this point, and guests begin to stream into the room, preventing Alice from replying even if she wanted to. *I took his phone. And wallet. And keys. And then abandoned him in the middle of London. Naked.*

Despite a hangover that makes the whole room feel like it's gently pulsating, Alice forces a cheery smile for the guests; busies herself ladling out bowls of steaming soup, and offering bread rolls to cold, hungry hands. She's so focused on the rhythm of pour-pass-smile that she barely even notices the people she's serving today, only realizes that one of them has stopped in front of her when he starts to speak. 'The AA meets here every Tuesday night.'

'Excuse me?' she replies.

'It's okay to ask for help. With your drinking problem.'

Other people in the queue begin to crane forward, though Alice can't tell if they're trying to listen in or simply want to know what the hold-up is.

'It's not what you think.'

'The first step to recovery is being truthful with yourself,' he says, moving down the line again. 'Your new life can only begin when you're ready to be honest.'

*

'So how did it go?' says Frida, as soon as the last of the guests have left.

'Oh, fine,' replies Alice, certain that this is not the time for truth.

'Chris was so excited about seeing you again. Am I allowed to tell you that? I wouldn't have said it beforehand, but it's okay now, isn't it? He's been like a kid at Christmas.'

'He is very sweet,' says Alice, feeling guiltier by the second.

'I'm glad you say that. Because he is sweet, he really is. He's just one of those people; he's got such a good heart, he deserves to be happy. So when will you be seeing each other again?'

Alice shrugs. 'I'm sure we'll talk at some point.'

'If you don't mind me saying, I get the feeling that you've had some bad experiences with men in your life. I'm no expert, but I think maybe you just need to take a chance on a good guy. And that's what Chris is, a really good guy.'

Brixton, London SW2
13 miles from Alice

Many more of Neville's feathers are missing by the time Ben gets home; the crest on his head and down his back in stark contrast to his increasingly bald body.

'I'm going to find you a new home,' says Ben. Unlike all the other times when he's stood in front of this cage, when he's viewed Neville as a burden, sometimes even a threat, now he feels only compassion; that if he can salvage this bird's life, he may yet be able to do good things for his own. 'It's going to be a proper home, with people who love you and understand you.' Perhaps sensing the change in Ben's tone, Neville peers at him from the corner of the cage. 'That's going to be my gift to you, Neville. A good home. And a long and happy life.'

Although he'd imagined it would be a Herculean task, Neville's salvation actually involves just a quick Google search and a phone call.

'It's true, parrots aren't for everyone,' says the woman at the parrot rescue charity, her patient voice – not to mention the incessant background squawking – suggesting that she under-stands the subject better than most. 'I'm sure we can find him a good home.'

'I wanted to look after him myself,' says Ben, certain that this is true in spirit if not in fact. 'He was my grandparents', you see. But I can't, he's just not happy, and every day it's worse, tearing his feathers out and looking like he wants to die.'

'I understand,' replies the woman in a soothing voice, seemingly familiar with people's need for confession and absolution. 'You're doing the right thing, I promise you that. Now, then...' He hears the flicking of pages, imagines that she's opening a big, heavy book of worthy parrot lovers, its pages radiating a golden light. 'Since it sounds like quite an urgent situation, how about I arrange for someone to come and collect him tomorrow?'

'So soon.'

'I can give you more time, if you like.'

Ben glances over at Neville, his patchy and dejected appearance a reminder that time is not on their side. 'No,' he says. 'Tomorrow is fine.'

*

Anyone would think it's a deathbed vigil, the way Ben spends the evening sitting by Neville's cage, the whole room flickering by candlelight while he tries to feed Neville his favourite foods.

'It's our last night together,' says Ben, no longer sure if this is a good thing or not. Perhaps out of a rising sense of hope, or merely in response to Ben's sadness, Neville takes a chunk of pineapple from between the bars. 'I'm sorry for hating you all these years. And I'm sure if you could talk, you'd apologize for hating me too.' Neville gives him a look that suggests otherwise, his beak now dripping with juice. 'It's odd, you could live for another sixty years. Even after I've died of old age, you'll probably still be going strong. And yet I might never see you again after tomorrow. I know you won't believe me, but I'm going to miss you.'

In reply, Neville cocks his head and gives Ben a gentle squawk, the closest he has ever come to sounding tender.

Brixton, London SW2

4 miles from Alice

'Keep your eyes closed,' says Dave, as he leads Ben out to the street.

'Have you bought me a Lamborghini?'

'If you're going to start the ride again, you're going to need a bike. So, ta-da!' Ben opens his eyes to find Agnes's bike chained to a lamppost. 'Since she won't be needing it for a while...'

'Oh, mate.'

'It's not the best bike, but—'

'No, it's a million times better than that piece of crap I had before.'

'*My* bike, you mean. The one that's now at the bottom of a river.'

'Turns out it's not a river; I looked it up online. It's a drainage channel.' He admires the bike in front of him. 'I would say this is better than a Lamborghini, but, of course, that wouldn't be true. To be honest, it's not second best either, because that would be a Ferrari. And if you factor in yachts and helicopters and supermodels, this bike is way, way down on the list. Probably like, I don't know, a hundred and ninety-three or something.'

'Ben...'

'But I love it. Thank you. That's what I was trying to say. It's wonderful, and I love it.'

'I do have one more surprise for you.' He beams like Santa Claus. 'Agnes's mum has agreed to lend me her car for the day, so when you're ready to get started, I can take you and the bike up there.'

'Can we go tomorrow?' Dave's smile fades. 'What I mean is, thank you, that's a very nice offer. And if it's at all possible, I would like to leave tomorrow. Please.'

*

While Ben makes them a cup of tea, Dave stands beside Neville's cage; he clearly wants to try Agnes's trick of rubbing the parrot's neck, but lacks the courage.

'It's funny,' he says. 'It's almost like he knows that he's leaving. He's even looking a bit better.' Ben brings him a mug of tea, the two of them standing there, watching Neville like a spectator sport. 'Not many people know this, but parrots are very intelligent. They have the IQ of a seven-year-old child.'

'Great,' replies Ben, 'he's cleverer than I am. It's no wonder he's hated me all these years.' Mug of tea in one hand, he uses the other to offer Neville a slice of apple. 'It's odd, it's only now that I'm about to say goodbye, I realize we could have been friends.' Neville snatches the apple from his fingers and throws it to the floor. 'Okay, perhaps not friends. But, you know, maybe we could have understood each other better.'

Head cocked, Neville regards him through one bulging eye.

'I think you'll find,' says Dave, 'Neville has always understood you completely.'

*

Neville departs with all the ease of a corn being removed – completely at odds with the long years that Ben has thought of him as a diseased organ, a virulent cancerous growth.

The man who comes to collect him appears to take it all in his stride; the way Neville has torn out so many feathers, he looks more like the victim of abuse than a cherished family pet.

'I wouldn't worry,' he says. 'They do that sometimes, the unhappy ones. It'll get better with time.'

And distance from me, thinks Ben.

It comes as some surprise when he realizes that the man has brought his own cage for transporting Neville; that Ben will be left with his grandmother's as a feathery, shit-encrusted reminder of his inability to look after another living thing.

Neville hops on to the man's hand with ill-concealed joy, much how Ben can imagine people rushing for the last helicopter out of a war zone. Moments later, he's safely in his new cage and ready to leave Ben's life forever.

'Do you think it would be possible to see some pictures of him from time to time?' says Ben.

'I don't see why not,' the man replies.

'I know my gran would like to see him happy.'

'And they do love to be admired,' he says, cooing over Neville. 'We'll get all that sorted in due course.'

Ben follows him out to the hallway, watches as they move towards the stairs. Neville, too, turns in his cage as if to say goodbye, two old foes with a shared history, their time together coming to an end. And as Ben stands there, watching Neville gaze back, he imagines how it will feel at the end of his life: how, as an old and wizened man, Ben will smile on his deathbed because somewhere out there Neville is still flapping happily around an aviary full of feathered friends.

Mayfair, London W1

With the party just days away, life in the office has taken on the feel of a bad acid trip, not helped by the day-glo colours of the client's product range. Having somehow survived the day, Alice tries to tell herself that dinner with her father will be a reward of sorts, but the words don't ring true; she's so

251

intent on asking for his help to buy a flat, it feels more like she's preparing for an important interview.

There's been no news all day from Rachel; the pressures of working life doubtless having distracted her, or perhaps even killed her outright. Even though Alice thinks of calling to make sure she's okay, it's Chris she rings on the way to the restaurant. Finding herself shunted through to voicemail yet again, she simply hangs up, unsure what to say anymore, but then regrets that too; regrets everything, in fact, the feeling growing so heavy that by the time she reaches the restaurant – a small Italian place near the Strand – it's impossible to imagine the evening going well.

By contrast, her father looks more relaxed than she's ever seen him before.

'You look amazing,' she says, as they sit down at their table, cosseted in a wood-panelled booth.

'I do feel rather good,' he replies. 'I've had a very pleasurable afternoon.'

'What were you doing?'

'Oh, this and that,' he says, blushing. 'All that matters is that life is beginning to open up in wonderful ways.'

'I'm still trying to get my head around seeing you in London. It makes such a change from the attic.'

'Believe it or not, I've stopped all that. I've decided to sell all the trains, sell the lot of it.' Alice stares at him, too shocked to respond. 'In many ways your mother was right. I was just wasting my life up there; gently hitting the bumpers on the sidings of existence.'

'Wow,' says Alice, still struggling to comprehend the news.

'I don't want you to be alarmed when I say this, but your mother and I have decided to live more... how shall I say? Freely.'

'And what does that mean, exactly?'

'Well, how honest do you want me to be?'

252

'Come on, Daddy, you can tell me anything, you know that.'

'Well, I want you to know that your mother and I still love each other very much…'

Still? thinks Alice. *When did you ever love each other?*

'… but we've both agreed it's the right time in our lives to cast the net wider, in every way. To fully enjoy the years we have left.' The words bring a smile to his face. 'If you'd told me even a few weeks ago that I'd be selling my trains, I would have said you're mad. It happened at the exhibition. I just woke up one morning and thought "I can't stand to go and tinker with those bloody things anymore". And it's not a cheap hobby, I'll tell you that. Certainly no cheaper than seeing a good prostitute once or twice a month.'

In the stunned silence that follows, Alice can think only of the lines she's rehearsed so many times in recent days. 'I wanted to talk with you about the future. My future.'

'Wonderful! Maybe I can get things rolling by cutting straight to the chase. The real reason I wanted us to meet is to discuss your inheritance.' He gives her a kindly smile. 'There won't be one. We've decided to spend the money on ourselves.'

'Nothing?' says Alice.

'The world's changed.'

'Yes, it's much more expensive.'

'Exactly, which is surely a sign of how well the economy's doing? The economy that you're now a part of, earning a salary.'

'But not one that will ever allow me to, I don't know, buy my own place, for instance.'

'Home ownership is overrated, Alice. Just look at the Germans. Most of them rent for their whole lives.'

'But this isn't Germany.'

'If it's any consolation, we're not really homeowners anymore either. I'm cashing in my pension and signing the house over to an equity company.' By now, Alice feels incapable of speech, just stares at him. 'You have to remember, in the olden days, your mother and I would be dead already, long since carried off by the Black Death or some such.' A waitress cuts between them with a basket of bread. She's barely put it down before Alice starts on it, in desperate need of a carbohydrate hug. 'What I'm trying to say,' her father continues, 'is that longer lives require a new way of managing finances.'

'So,' she replies, through a full mouth, 'just to be clear on this, I'm not going to inherit anything because there's no Black Death in Essex?'

'Someone has to pay for our retirement. I would rather it be us than you.'

'But if you're spending my inheritance, it *is* me.'

'Yes, yes, I see your point, but let's be brutally honest. You can't miss what you've never had. And this way, circumstances will inspire you to spread your wings and fly.' He gives her another smile. 'Trust me, it's better this way. Better for everyone. I would even go so far as to say that your mother and I have never been happier than we are right now.' He watches as Alice eats yet more of the bread. 'Is it good?'

'I honestly don't know,' she says, spitting crumbs on the tablecloth. 'I don't even care.'

Her father seems unfazed. 'And what was it that you wanted to discuss with me?'

'It's nothing,' she mumbles, already reaching for more bread. 'Forget I even mentioned it.'

Day

27

Tuesday

The M1, heading north

27 miles from Alice and counting

Dave failed to mention that Agnes's mother drives an old Fiat 500, so that the bike essentially fills the entire space, forcing Dave and Ben to fit around it as best they can. The engine turns out to be equally petite, the two of them travelling on the motorway at an almost ceremonial pace, while an endless stream of vehicles tears past.

Ben holds his grandfather's urn on his lap. 'This speed would make sense if he was still in a coffin.'

'Slow and steady wins the race,' replies Dave, eyes fixed on the road ahead.

'You wouldn't say that if you were in a Porsche.' Ben watches a coachload of old people overtake them. 'They'll probably all be dead by the time we get there.'

'Ben, the car, like all of us, has its limits.'

'Don't worry, mate, it's not a criticism. I like watching the world go by.' More cars and trucks zoom past. 'And it really is going by, isn't it? So much faster than us.'

'Tell me about your plans for the next few days,' says Dave, his tone making it clear that he wants to change the subject.

'Thers's not much to tell. I'm going to spend the rest of the day looking around Matlock. When we finally get there.'

Dave takes a deep breath, says nothing. Off to their right

is the monotone sprawl of Luton; a tubercular gob of phlegm in concrete and glass. 'I envy you, getting away from all this.'

'Then stay with me for a day or two.'

'I wish. Agnes's mum needs the car first thing in the morning.'

'What's she going to do with it? Mow the lawn?'

Dave tightens his grip on the steering wheel. 'You still haven't told me your plans for the rest of the week.'

'I'm just going to set off from Matlock and cycle about in the Peak District for a bit.'

'You don't have a route in mind?'

Ben gives the urn an affectionate pat. 'We'll just drift with the landscape and go wherever looks pretty.'

Oxford Street, London W1

With Chris still not speaking to her, Alice spends her lunchtime trying to find him a gift. Never mind that it would already be a challenge to buy something for a man she barely knows, this gift also needs to be apologetic, charming, seductive and totally vegan. These complex criteria eliminate everything she can think of, leaving her aimless on Oxford Street, surrounded by a million possibilities, but convinced that none of them are right. There's a brief moment when she considers a teddy bear, but then decides that it's too much like a voodoo doll; that she may as well stick a photo of herself on its face and send it to Chris with a box of pins.

Adrift in the lunchtime crowd, and still unsure what to buy him, Alice decides to call Rachel. She's thinking of what excuse she can give for not calling sooner when Rachel beats her to it. 'Sorry for the silence,' she says to Alice. 'I should have at least texted you yesterday, but there are no emojis to express how awful my job is.'

'It'll get better.'

'No, it won't. It's not a career, it's a hostage crisis. Every time I think things have hit a new low, I remember it's going to be another forty years until I can retire.'

'But you're on your way now. Give it enough time and you'll…' She pauses, unsure what the career path is for someone who works in fast food. 'You'll work your way up to something well-paid.'

'As far as I can tell, that basically involves barking at people who earn minimum wage.'

'But with a guaranteed supply of empty calories for the rest of your life.'

'True. And a boss who isn't trying to sleep with me.'

'See, you're living the dream, you just haven't realized it yet.'

'And how are you?'

Disinherited. Sad. Confused. 'I'm fine. Just out doing some shopping.'

'Anything special?'

A man passes with a bunch of flowers; a colourful beacon of forgiveness, romance, hope. 'Er, not really,' she replies. 'Just this and that.' She turns to watch him go, the flowers bobbing in front of him like some blazing torch. 'Sorry, I've just realized there's something I need to get. I'll call you later.'

*

It's only when Alice is back in the office, browsing the website of a local florist, that she begins to worry all over again: Chris would surely want something more sustainable than cut flowers, the blooms only consuming water as part of some slow, protracted death.

She's still agonizing over her options when she turns to find both Geneva and Harry right behind her, staring at her computer screen. Even Harry looks judgemental, as though he finds the arrangements cheap and artless. 'So,' says Geneva, 'buying someone flowers, eh?'

'I'm not getting any of these,' replies Alice. 'I think a potted plant is the right choice.'

'I don't know how things are in your world, but it's normally other people buying *me* flowers.'

'Well, these are special circumstances.'

'Do I sense an interesting story?'

'No.'

'Our very own Miss Sunshine being evasive. Curiouser and curiouser.'

Reluctant to call the florist while Geneva is in earshot, Alice waits for her to inevitably grow bored of work. As soon as she wanders away to terrorize people elsewhere in the office, Alice lunges for her phone.

'I want to order a potted plant,' she says. 'Can you deliver to Woolwich?'

In the minutes that follow, the woman at the other end tries to describe her available stock, the conversation quickly becoming mired in the intricacies of sunlight, shade, thirst and maintenance. Geneva is already returning to her desk by the time that Alice has decided on a cactus.

'Yes, that's right, a cactus,' she says, trying to hurry the conversation along. 'Preferably one with flowers.' Even though Geneva is now listening, Alice is still pleased with the choice: never mind that it's covered in thorns, it's a living organism, a paragon of virtue when it comes to water consumption, and the flowers will surely be a reminder that good things can blossom from even the harshest circumstances.

As soon as the call is finished, Geneva speaks. 'Sending a gift to another man. What would Ben say?'

'If he knew all the details, I'm sure he'd approve. Chris is just… a friend.'

'Alice, if a cactus is the kind of thing you give to a friend, I'd hate to see what you send to your enemies.'

'It is quite an expensive cactus.'

'But a cactus nevertheless. Why even bother having it delivered? Why not just tie it to something heavy and throw it through his window?' Deciding to say nothing, Alice pretends to busy herself with work. 'And *still* no reaction. Not even the slightest irritation with anything I say.'

'You're entitled to your opinion.'

'You'd never hear *me* say something like that.'

'I'd like to think I can always find something positive to say.'

'Yes, of course you can,' says Geneva, clearly not intending it as a compliment. 'Once again, you get ten out of ten for being Little Miss Optimistic. Though not for the first time, Alice, I just wonder where the rest of you is.'

Derbyshire
119 miles from Alice and counting

When the southernmost edges of the Peak District come into view – dancing in a distant haze like some trick of the light – it's as much as Ben can do not to take the urn and hold it up to the window. Even though his grandfather was a man of few words, it's hard to imagine him staying silent in the presence of that view: the upward thrust of the land enough to make all human experience seem less important, all memories less painful. Ben watches, mesmerized, as they slowly get closer, the land rising as if to wrap them in a warm embrace.

'At least stay for a cup of tea,' says Ben, as they arrive in Matlock.

'I swear, if I get out of this car now I'll never want to get back in.'

Dave pulls to a stop beside the river, the town appearing like a hidden nook: stone cottages tumbling down the hillside, the whole place hidden in a thick, wooded fold of the land.

'Well, okay, then,' says Ben. 'Goodbye.'

'There's no need to make it sound so final.'

'Sorry, it's just, you know.' He nods at the urn, still on his lap. 'There's a thin line between life and death, isn't there?'

'Mate, you definitely need a cup of tea. With a couple of extra sugars.'

He's barely finished speaking when Ben reaches over and gives him a hug, the urn pressed between them. 'Be careful on the roads.'

'It's not me on a bicycle.'

'I'll let you know how I'm getting on. I'll phone and send postcards and stuff.'

'More importantly, come home with tales to tell your godchild.' He gives Ben a fond smile. 'And now get your bike and piss off, before my resolve weakens.'

*

It's odd at first, having the urn in his backpack, the weight of it tugging at his shoulder like an excited child, Ben and his grandfather out together on a big adventure. Thinking that his granddad would have liked to see Matlock, they wander the narrow streets together, and even ride the cable car up to the Heights of Abraham, all the while Ben making one-sided observations about the view and the weather.

As charming as the village is, it still feels good to leave it. With a gentle push he's off, slicing through the warm air of a sunny afternoon; past the idling tour buses, and the geraniums in window boxes. As he leaves the village behind, it's a struggle at first, climbing into the hills, every turn of the pedals a reminder that gravity is not in his favour. And yet he can't stop and push the bike, not on the first ride with his grandfather, not with the ashes of a man who lived through war and starvation and torture. And so he keeps going, slowly gaining height while his legs burn beneath him.

By the time the road begins to level out, it feels like he's exactly where he should be, doing precisely what he should be doing. There's a hypnotic quality to this place: the landscape rising and falling all around him while he beats out a steady rhythm on the pedals. As he crests another hill, the wind is on his back and it feels as though this bike, these legs, are super-charged; that they could, in fact, propel him to anywhere in the world if only given the time.

The Peak District
134 miles from Alice

When Ben first opens his eyes, the smell of bacon drifting from the kitchen is so redolent of home, he half expects to hear Dave bursting into song at any moment. But then he starts to notice other details: how the bed is so much bigger and more comfortable than the one he has in London; how the only sound from outside is birdsong. And then memories of the previous day come flooding back: how he'd enjoyed the ride so much, he didn't even keep track of where he was; how nightfall reduced the landscape to a small pool of light from his bicycle headlamp, and yet still he'd kept going, intoxicated by the spinning of the wheels beneath him and the freedom of the open road.

Choosing this bed and breakfast had been a random act – part happenstance, part desperation – and yet, as he'd ridden down the rutted driveway, it seemed faintly magical: the windows of the farmhouse glowing against the night sky, nothing to break the silence except the distant call of owls hunting in the darkness.

*

It's only as he heads downstairs that he realizes how stiff his legs are; the creaking of the oak staircase seeming to echo his physical state. He's not even reached the bottom when a door in the hallway swings open and a middle-aged woman pops into view.

'Good morning,' she says, so cheerful that it's impossible to imagine the day being anything other than good. 'We normally serve breakfast in the dining room, but you're our only guest at the moment, so you're welcome to come and eat with us, if you like.' He follows her into the kitchen, the air heavy with the scents of toast and bacon. 'Are you feeling a bit stiff from your ride?'

'Like I've spent days being probed by aliens.'

'Well, I don't recall seeing any spaceships last night,' she replies, with a laugh. 'So I daresay you're just saddle sore.' She's still chuckling to herself when the back door opens and her husband enters, the same man who showed Ben to his room last night. She calls to him without even looking in his direction. 'Take your boots off, Jeff.'

He backtracks to the doormat, winks at Ben as he pulls them off. 'I see you've met *mein Führer*.'

'But you can call me Karen,' she says to Ben. 'I'm afraid my husband spends most of his time with sheep, so he doesn't have great social skills.' Ben watches as Jeff crosses the room, in socked feet now, and gives her an affectionate kiss. 'Too bad he often smells like sheep too.'

Jeff takes a seat opposite Ben. 'Will you be cycling far?'

'I'm not sure yet. Originally, I was riding to Glasgow, but, er, it's a long story.'

'So you're footloose and fancy free?' says Jeff.

'Yeah, basically. The idea is to just spend some time with my granddad; show him around a bit.'

'How lovely,' says Karen. 'Where's he staying?'

'He's up in my room, sitting on the window ledge.' He notices their confusion. 'I've got his ashes in an urn. It means the conversation's a bit limited, but to be honest that was always the case, even when he was alive.' He watches as Karen starts laying out his breakfast. 'Do you need a hand with all that?'

'No, thanks. I know I'm probably setting feminism back a generation, but the truth is I like to fuss.' She puts yet more food on the table. 'I like seeing people well-fed.'

'By which she means overweight,' says Jeff.

Ben stares at the growing mountain of food in front of him. 'And comatose.'

'Nonsense,' she replies. 'You're young enough that you'll have burnt it all off by lunchtime. And as for my husband here…' She turns to him and pretends to look stern. 'I'm hoping a big breakfast might give him the energy to finally do some of the things that need fixing around the house.'

Mayfair, London W1

The first that Alice hears of her mother's visit is when she calls at eleven o'clock in the morning. 'Darling, I'm in town today. Let's have lunch.'

'Could you not have given me more warning?'

'Alice,' she says, doubtless trying to sound jovial, but failing. 'You need to be more spontaneous. I've always thought that about you.'

'Do you even know how to find my office?'

'I thought it would be more theatrical if we met on the steps of St Paul's.'

'I don't work anywhere near there.'

'Alice, how often do I come into London? This is a special occasion. And remember, spontaneity is the new word of the day.'

*

When Alice reaches St Paul's, she finds her mother looking uncharacteristically relaxed; is greeted with the kind of genuinely happy smile that Alice has never seen on her before.

'I'm so glad you could make it,' she says, the words even

269

sounding sincere. 'I should have called you earlier, but the whole trip was very spur of the moment.'

'I can't remember the last time you came into town.'

'When you're older, you'll understand that life often gets in the way of pleasure. But now that your father and I have made some changes…' There's a subtle shift in her expression. 'He told me you took the news very well.'

Alice attempts a smile she doesn't feel. 'I want to see the two of you happy.'

'And we are, like never before.' She takes a deep breath, appears to savour the gritty urban air. 'I feel alive again. I think we should celebrate with a glass of wine.'

'I thought we were having lunch?'

'We *can*,' she says, dragging the word out until it's on its knees, begging for more syllables. 'But it might be nice to have a glass of wine first, don't you think? It'll give us some time to think about where to go.'

'I only have an hour.'

'Then just take longer. Tell your boss that your mother's in town.'

'If you could meet these people, you'd realize that my personal happiness is not high on their list of priorities.'

Her mother hooks her arm in Alice's, starts leading her away. 'It's my treat, and I'm not going to let anyone get in my way. If they have a problem with it, you can send them to me.'

*

In the fifteen minutes that it takes her mother to have first one glass of wine and then another, it becomes clear to Alice that she's after an audience, not company; that they're not spending time together because of bonds of kinship, but rather because Alice is the only person her mother has for this purpose: an unpaid extra, always ready for a walk-on role.

'I don't remember you drinking this much,' says Alice.

'You can blame your father for that,' she replies, a sparkle in her eye.

'And that too. Talking about him in a… a *playful* way. It's hard to get used to.'

'Alice, you make it sound like we hate each other. We've been married for thirty years, we must have been doing something right.' Another sip of wine. 'You should have had a glass yourself, it would help you relax.'

'Work is really busy at the moment. We've got this huge party coming up on Friday.'

'That sounds like fun.'

'Mother, we're the organizers, not the guests. The way it's going, the whole thing will be like crawling across broken glass.'

'You should ask Ben to give you a massage. How is he?'

An elaborate fiction. A lie. 'He's fine,' she replies, glancing at her watch.

'Look, I don't want to keep you. How about we just skip lunch and do a bit of shopping instead?'

'I have thirty minutes left, if we leave right now.'

'That's plenty,' she says, downing the last of her wine. 'You probably don't know it, but you're looking at one of the world's greatest power shoppers.'

*

They take a cab back across to the West End, Alice's mother unable to conceal her joy as they pull up in front of Selfridges.

'Mother, I don't have any time left.'

'Your office is just around the corner. Give me ten more minutes and then you're free to go.' She leads the way, Moses-like, across the crowded pavement and through the heavy doors into the fragrant embrace of the perfume hall. 'Your father and I are planning a holiday,' she says, as they head for the escalators. 'I think some new swimwear is in order. How about one for me, and one for you? My treat.'

271

'Where are you and Dad going?'

'We're not sure yet, but I'd like one of those all-inclusive resorts, maybe in Barbados. I can just sit on the beach and drink cocktails all day.' They ride each escalator in silence, carried upwards three floors into a world of women's wear. As they're finally spewed into a sea of this season's must-have items, she speaks again. 'What would you think if I got a facelift and joined Twitter?' Alice says nothing, her mother scuttling after her. 'You don't approve, do you?'

'It's your money,' replies Alice, heading for the swimwear. 'You and Dad are entitled to do as you please.'

'Well, now that you mention it, I was wondering…' She lowers her voice to an indiscreet whisper. 'Do you know where I can buy some cocaine?'

'Mother!'

'What? You're young.'

'Yes, which means I spend my entire salary, if you can even call it that, on rent and train fares and whatever's on discount at the supermarket. And the thing is, even if I wasn't merely *existing*, I wouldn't be spending my money on drugs.'

'For Christ's sake, Alice, you're only twenty-two. If I'd met you at your age, I would have thought you very boring.'

'I'm a little confused why you and Dad would rather throw your money away than lend me a hand.'

Her mother doesn't even look at her as she speaks, is too busy checking a skimpy swimsuit. 'Darling, you can't expect to be given everything on a platter.'

'Why not? Your generation was.'

'I think you'll find we built this society, thank you very much.'

Alice snaps at her. 'No, Mother, that was your parents and grandparents.'

Her mother looks up, smiling. 'I know why you're so tetchy!

You've had a fight with Ben, haven't you?' She goes back to rummaging through the rack. 'You've always been like that; throwing your toys from the pram just because no one wanted to touch you.' She holds up a garish blue tankini. 'What do you think of this one?'

'It's not my colour.'

'Not for *you*, darling, for me.' She laughs to herself. 'You'd need to lose more than a few pounds before you could wear something like that.'

The Peak District
136 miles from Alice

'This is more work than I expected,' says Ben.

'There's never a dull day,' replies Jeff, shouting over the sound of his old Land Rover. He points to yet more fields, the landscape dotted with sheep. 'That's all ours too.'

'How do you keep track of it all?'

'It's a full-time job, that's for sure. And our lambing season is coming up, which is a hundred times busier.'

'And you do it all on your own?'

'I used to have someone helping out, but he moved on. The winters can be harsh up here. It's not the life for everyone.'

'We have winters in London too, but we don't have views like this.'

'If you think this is good, just you wait.' He turns the car uphill and accelerates across the open pasture.

The vehicle begins to shake and rattle, the noise growing so violent that Ben's certain the whole car will start to disintegrate at any second. 'I feel like we're about to go into orbit,' he shouts.

Jeff accelerates yet more, Ben holding tight as the rattling grows louder and louder. Moments later they're cresting the

273

hill, the land sweeping down in every direction. Jeff pulls to an abrupt stop, the roar of the engine giving way to nothing but the sound of the wind.

'Bloody hell,' says Ben, looking first this way and then that. 'We really are in orbit.'

'It's a special place, isn't it? I find any excuse I can to come up here.'

They get out of the car, the wind tugging at their hair, their clothes. 'I can see now why my granddad always wanted to come here.'

'I'm sure he'd be thrilled to know that you went to all the trouble of bringing him.'

'It's funny, I've spent more time talking to him in an urn than I ever did when he was alive.'

'I have no idea what happens when we're gone,' Jeff says, looking out at the landscape. 'But I'd like to think that, somewhere out there, your grandfather isn't just listening to you, he's loving every moment of it.'

★

When Ben eventually goes to bed that night, he takes his grandfather's urn from the window ledge and puts it on the bedside table.

'I hope you've enjoyed the day,' he says. 'I didn't mean to leave you alone up here, but you've had a nice view.' He stares at the urn, thinking of the man inside. 'And you don't have to worry about anything anymore. You're safe with me. Just like I was always safe with you.'

Smiling at the thought, he turns off the light, the faint silhouette of his grandfather still visible in the gloom: companion, protector, friend.

He's just closed his eyes, still smiling to himself, when he hears Alice's voice. 'It's time for a goodnight kiss.'

He finds her sitting on the edge of his bed, leaning in to kiss him on the forehead.

'You're not real,' he shouts, yanking the bedcover over his face. 'This is all in my imagination.'

'If I'm not real, why are you hiding?'

He pokes his head out. 'I know you're not Alice.'

'I never said I was Alice. You did.'

'You're not my mother either.'

'But you'd like me to be your mother, wouldn't you?' She gives him such a smile that, for a moment, it's true.

'Oh, God,' he says, ducking back under the blanket. 'This is even worse than I thought. I need different medication. And more of it. Much, much more of it.'

'Is there something you want to tell me, Ben? I think there is.'

'This isn't happening. My mother's dead. You're not real.'

'I know what you want to tell me.'

Ben starts to shout, drowning her out. 'La la la la la la la...'

He's still shouting when he hears a knock on his bedroom door, Jeff calling to him. 'Is everything all right in there?'

Ben pulls back the blanket to find that Alice has gone; nothing but him and his grandfather alone in the darkness.

The 08:05 to London Waterloo

The way Alice feels today, she hasn't simply woken up on the wrong side of bed, she's woken up on the wrong side of reality. Heading for Waterloo on a crowded train, it seems like every other person on board knows something about life that she doesn't; some magic password that gives them the strength to make it through another day.

The memory of yesterday still rings in her ears: the casual put-downs that come so naturally to her mother – and, all the while, Alice biting her tongue, trying to be the one who rises above provocation; the person who can always find something positive in even the worst situations. And in that moment it strikes how her cruel everyday life can be: that she is starving and yet fat; employed and yet poor; kind to others and yet…

She closes her eyes, tries to imagine a long list of all the things that make her loveable – a river of words that will confirm she's deserving of happiness – but all she can picture is a blank page.

Reasons I'm grateful…

This seems a safer list. Sure enough, it's easy to think of some basics: she's grateful, for instance, that the train has wheels; that they're actually turning this morning. But a list like that is not enough, not today.

Things I like about myself...

    1. **I can always find something positive to say!**

    2. **Even when I've been knocked down, I always get back up.**

Never mind that the words speak volumes about the other people in her life, at least they're something.

Feeling a little better, she starts to consider her physical attributes and immediately feels the momentum slow. It takes some time before she can think of anything.

    3. **I quite like the colour of my eyes.**

How much easier it would be if she was making a list of the things she *doesn't* like: the way her ankles look in high heels; the way her hair seems to have a mind of its own, but insufficient intelligence to make the right decisions.

The train is just leaving Putney when she glances down at the man sitting in front of her, an open magazine in his hands. And then she sees the headline. *10 Weeks to the Perfect Beach Body.*

'Oh, fuck off,' she says, the words coming out like a knee jerk, something beyond her control.

He looks up. 'Excuse me?'

On any other day, she'd just apologize and spend the rest of the journey blushing, but as she looks at it a second time, she can feel the anger rising. 'That headline. It's total bollocks.'

'Calm down,' he mutters, already starting to read again, 'it's only a magazine.'

'But it's not, is it? It's body-shaming propaganda designed to make people feel bad about themselves. Surely a beach body is just a body on a beach?'

He glances at her waistline. 'You might do better by reading it yourself.'

'What did you say?' As her pitch rises, Alice notices that

other passengers are now looking at her, but she can't stop herself, the words spuming forth in ever-higher octaves. 'Why should I feel bad about my body just because it's not your idea of perfection? It belongs to me, not you.'

A different passenger speaks, a woman. 'If it's any consolation, I think you've lost a little weight recently.'

'I don't even know who you are,' says Alice. 'And even though it's a very sweet thing to say, and I would have taken it as a compliment until about sixty seconds ago, now I think why should I? If we're supposed to feel better about ourselves when we lose weight, what's the opposite? Should we hang our heads in shame if we gain five pounds?'

The man with the magazine speaks again. 'That might be a better strategy than just eating another cake.'

'Okay, that's it,' she says, beginning to unbutton her coat and untuck her blouse. '*This* is a beach body…'

The man turns away. 'You shouldn't do that.'

'Sorry, I'm not going to do anything any more just because you or anyone else wants me too.' She pulls up her clothes to reveal a slab of pale belly fat. 'Ta-da! A beach body!' She turns to the rest of the carriage. 'And I've just decided that I'm going to stop dieting! Until this morning, you could have told me about the "bleed through your eyes diet" and I would have been like "Ooh, does it work?" Well, no more! And for the record, I am completely happy the way I am. In fact, it's only now that I think about it, I've *always* felt okay about being overweight, it's everyone else who seems to have a problem with it.' By now the whole carriage is looking at her, their faces a sea of interest, concern, judgement. 'Also, for the record, I have a patch of scaly skin just here.' She pulls her blouse even higher. 'Right here under my left boob. And as from this moment, I don't care about that either.' She turns again, so yet more passengers can see. 'I'm also going to buy a bikini today and, as soon as it's warm enough, I'm going to wear it *on the beach*.' She lets go of her blouse, unaware that it's still snagged on her bra, her mind racing with all the other things that are wrong with existence. 'I'd also like to point out,' she says, shouting to the whole carriage, 'my mother's generation did not build the modern world. They *inherited* a prosperous society, and then systematically stripped it of all its resources, without any thought for the consequences.' Hearing someone groan, she raises her voice yet further. 'And don't even get me started on unpaid internships. It's not a career path, it's social cleansing.' She realizes that the handsome man of mystery is in the crowd staring back at her. 'This is probably the wrong moment,' she says, to him. 'But I just want you to know, you are a very attractive man. A very, *very* attractive man.'

'I'm gay,' he replies.

'Of course you are! It's so obvious!' He looks offended now. 'What I mean is, I'm a big supporter of gay rights. Go you!' In the long, awkward silence that follows – eighty or ninety people staring at her – Alice realizes that her blouse is still up, her bra still visible, her bare belly flab wobbling with every movement. 'I think this is my stop,' she says, as the train pulls into Clapham Junction.

'This isn't Waterloo,' says yet another person whom Alice has never seen before.

'I'm not going to Waterloo.'

'But you always do.'

'Well, not today!' she says, opening the door.

Conscious that everyone in the carriage is still watching her, she walks away with what she hopes is a purposeful, self-possessed stride.

Someone else shouts to her. 'The exit's in the other direction.'

Alice turns, trying to preserve her carefree smile. 'Thank you,' she replies, avoiding all eye contact as she says it, certain that if she was to glance sideways right now, she would find a sea of faces watching her pass.

The Peak District
134 miles from Alice

Technically, it's work, and yet somehow the act of helping out on the farm is so enjoyable it's hard to think of it that way. For yet another day, Ben's grandfather sits on the window ledge, the landscape of the Peak District laid out before him, while Ben helps Jeff with his tasks.

'So everything was all right last night?' says Jeff, the two of them pitching hay in the sheep shed.

'Yeah, I was just…' *Seeing things. Hearing voices. Losing my mind.* 'I was in a car crash when I was young. I think it messed up my mind a bit.'

'Don't you worry about that. All that matters is you're okay. Much worse things can come from a car crash.'

'My mum and dad died in it.'

Jeff stops working. 'I'm sorry to hear that.'

'I was only five. I'm not sure if being so young made it better or worse. But I have a picture of my mother. I can show you later, if you like. She was very beautiful.'

'That'd be lovely. I'd be honoured to see it.'

They start working again, Jeff occasionally glancing at Ben with a kindly smile. 'I hope I'm not working you too hard,' he says.

'No, it's fun. I could get used to it.'

'It looks like you already have! I'd love to see what you make of lambing season. It's manic, but I can tell you now, it's the best feeling in the world.'

'It sounds amazing.'

'I was, er, thinking,' he says, trying a little too hard to make it sound offhand. 'You could stay around for a while. Longer than just a few days.'

'I couldn't afford to.'

'But you're not a guest anymore, you're a worker. It's only fair that you get all your board and lodging for free. And if you still like it after a few days, we can talk about a more official arrangement.'

It takes Ben a few seconds to understand what he's saying. 'Are you offering me a job?'

'There's always work to be done, you've seen that. And two pairs of hands make a big difference.' He suddenly looks shy, as if he's said too much. 'But there's no need to make a decision right now. You should take a few days to explore the area. I think you'll love it round here.'

Feltham, West London

Since mashed potato is the only thing on the menu, it would be wrong to say that Alice has invited Rachel to dinner. In truth, she's invited Rachel over to watch while she comfort-eats on an industrial scale.

'I can never take the train to work ever again,' she tells Rachel, as soon as she opens the front door. 'Never ever. I'm going to have to take the bus from now on or, I don't know, buy a bike.'

'What happened?' replies Rachel, as Alice shuffles back towards the kitchen in her slippers, Justin Bieber smiling up at her from each foot.

'Oh, God, I don't even know where to start. I think it's enough to say that a hundred strangers now know that I'm prone to belly button fluff.' She carries a large saucepan of mashed potato to the kitchen table, sits down with a fork.

'Alice, you can't eat five pounds of mashed potato.'

'I think you'll find I can,' she says, taking her first mouthful.

'Fine, what I mean is, don't. Knowing you, there's enough butter in there to euthanize a horse.'

'Then it's probably best you don't ask what's for dessert.' She takes another forkful. 'Anyway, you should be happy to see me eating. And there won't be any more diets either. That's the only good thing about all of this; I'm just going to be me from now on. Not that *that's* anything to celebrate.' She takes another scoop of potato. 'Even though today was an epic fail, it's just a small part of some much larger pattern of total crapness.'

Rachel takes a moment to respond. 'You have all the pieces of the puzzle, you're just trying to put them together in the wrong order.'

Alice stops eating, her fork hovering over the pot. 'Since when did you get so philosophical?'

'We're launching a new Sichuan chicken burger. I've been snacking on fortune cookies.'

'Oh, God, let's not talk about work. I didn't even go in today. Tomorrow is like the biggest event of the year, and I didn't go to work. I'll probably be fired.'

'Maybe you want to be fired.'

'Did you read that in a fortune cookie too?'

'No, Alice, they're supposed to be uplifting.'

'So nothing like "Your husband is sleeping with your best friend"? Or "You'll never find true love".' She takes a bigger mouthful of potato; fights the urge to just scoop it up with her bare hands. '"Your house will burn down tomorrow". "You'll always be stupid and ugly, and you'll die doing a job you hate".'

Rachel lifts away the pot. 'All right, that's enough. Each of us is allowed to wallow in self-pity for a specific amount of time, and yours has just run out.'

'Said the woman who hates everything about her life.'

'Fine, but at least I'm keeping my dream alive. Dreams are like flowers; they blossom when they're ready.' She looks self-conscious. 'Okay, yes, I got that from a fortune cookie, but it's good advice.' Perhaps finding the pot heavier than she expected, she puts it back on the table, pushes it out of Alice's reach. 'Look, let's be objective about this. Yes, your job sucks. Yes, you're likely to be poor for years to come. Yes, it sounds like you humiliated yourself in front of hundreds of people today.'

'Thank you for the reminder.'

'And let's not forget that every time you're interested in a man it ends up as some kind of charred, twisted wreckage.'

'Is this really supposed to be a pep talk?'

'My point is, you still have me.' She looks more excited now. 'I've been thinking, maybe one day I'll diversify my brand into a chain of musical burger joints.' She starts to sing. 'Why just have a cheeseburger when you can have a cheeeeesebuuuurrrrrrrrrger.'

'It's inspired,' says Alice, wanting only to put the mashed potato in her ears now.

'See, that's what I'm trying to tell you. The future is full of wonderful things. All you have to do is wait for it to open up like a flower.'

The Peak District
134 miles from Alice

Ben remains by the living room fire long after Jeff and Karen have gone to bed, the house dark and silent while he stares into the flames. He's so engrossed, he doesn't notice Alice at first, sitting in the shadows on the other side of the room.

'Ben,' she says, softly. 'I'm sorry for dying.'

'You're not real,' says Ben, angrily. 'None of this is real.'

He gets up and hurries from the room, starts to climb the stairs, but finds Alice is already standing at the top. 'We need to talk, Ben.'

He shouts up at her. 'Why won't you just leave me alone?'

'Because there are things we need to discuss.'

'I'm not going to have a chat with some figment of my imagination.' He heads for the kitchen instead, but as he flicks on the light, he discovers that Alice is in there too.

'Would you like a cup of tea?' she says.

'Leave me alone,' he bellows.

'I could make a cake.'

Ben lunges for the back door, unaware that upstairs lights are already turning on. Outside, the dogs start to bark as he runs across the farmyard and out into the darkness of the fields beyond. His mind is racing so fast, he doesn't even hear Jeff calling to him as he begins to climb uphill; doesn't see the small pool of torchlight that starts to follow him.

*

Ben doesn't stop until he reaches the summit, his breathing heavy in the cold night air, the wind gently stirring around him.

Jeff catches up with him a few minutes later, turning off his torch as he reaches Ben's side. 'I'd never thought of coming up here in the dark. It's rather lovely, isn't it?'

'Sorry if I woke you up.'

'Would you like to talk about it?'

'You'll think I'm mad.'

'Ben, if you've got something on your mind, I'll think you're human, that's all.'

'I've, er, been seeing something. Some*one*, actually.' He glances at Jeff, expects to see shock, horror, fear, but there's only the same look of gentle patience. 'I know it's all in my head, it's just she's been appearing for the last few weeks, and now she's insisting that we talk.'

'Maybe you should.'

'You're encouraging me to talk to an imaginary person?'

'I don't see why not.'

'Honestly, this has never happened to me before. I'm on meds, I don't mind admitting that, but there's never been anything like this.'

'Then it sounds like all the more reason to ask this person what she wants.'

'See, now you're going mad too.'

'The mind has funny ways of telling us things, Ben. I suspect it's not listening that drives a person to madness; it's hearing those things and trying to ignore them.'

Feltham, West London

Alice makes two depressing observations before she's even got out of bed. One, Chris still hasn't been back in touch, not even to acknowledge the cactus – not even to say *What the fuck? A cactus? REALLY?*, which under the circumstances would be a step forward in their relationship. Two, she has woken up considerably earlier than normal purely so she can take a different train to work, and as she lies there remembering why this is necessary, she realizes that she'll either have to move to a totally different part of London or keep doing this for the rest of her life.

*

When she gets to work, no one in the office asks why she was away yesterday. It's as though one look at her is enough to know that she has a genuine problem; if not a sickness of the body, then a sickness of the spirit.

'Are we all ready for the big night?' says Geneva, also in the office earlier than normal.

'I think so. Did I miss anything important yesterday?'

'What a ridiculous question. Of course not.' She hesitates a moment, looking at Alice with a more studied expression. 'It's going to be a late night. Are you sure you have the stamina for it?'

'I'm fine.'

'Of course you are,' she replies. 'Everything is always perfect in Alice's wonderland. Even when that's patently untrue.'

The Peak District
139 miles from Alice

Ben cycles along quiet country lanes, his grandfather a reassuring presence in his backpack; the two of them out together on another adventure, free to explore at their own pace; uphill stretches to challenge the legs, and freewheeling down the other side as a hard-won reward.

It's around midday when Ben sees a ridge looming in the distance, and instantly he knows that he must go up there, no matter how much effort is required. Merely trying to reach the bottom of the hill is a circuitous process, following lanes left and right, slowly zigzagging across the landscape. Even once he's there, finding a pathway is more a matter of luck than intuition, but still there's a sense of accomplishment as he locks his bike and begins to walk, climbing higher and higher past dry stone walls that look as old as the land itself.

It's mid-afternoon by the time he reaches the top, his breathing the only sound. He stands on the edge of the ridge, the green patchwork of the Peak District laid out beneath him. 'It's amazing, isn't it?' he says, no longer sure if he's talking to his grandfather or himself. 'It's your place, that's what it is. It's where you belong.'

He moves further along the ridge, hopping from rock to rock, unconcerned by the steep drop just inches to his left. Reaching a broad flat spot, he sits down, legs hanging over the precipice. 'I'd say this is a good spot for a late lunch, wouldn't you?' As he takes the urn and some sandwiches from his bag, he smiles at the thought of what his grandfather might say if only he was there in the flesh; how this man of so few words would probably be chattering like an excited child, the view powerful enough to work its magic even on him.

He's in the middle of eating when Alice sits down beside him, her bright yellow dress puffing out like a silken parachute.

Fighting the urge to say something, instead Ben focuses on finishing the rest of his sandwich, the two of them sitting there in silence.

'Just for the record,' he says, wiping the crumbs from his mouth, 'I know I'm talking to myself. You're not Alice, you're not my mother, you're me.'

'Inasmuch as I'm made from your memories of your mother, I am her. Those memories were always up there, Ben, hidden away in your mind; you just couldn't find them until you met Alice.'

'Yeah, well, it's still weird.'

'We can sing a song, if it would make you feel better.'

'No,' he says, abruptly, then softens his tone. 'No, thank you.' He glances around, worried that even up here someone may stumble across him in the middle of a monologue. 'It's true what you said last night. I've often wondered what I'd say if I could meet you. I mean, the real you, of course.'

She smiles at him, so warm, so tender, he can almost imagine how it must have been as a young child, gazing up at his mother, thinking her the most beautiful woman in the world. 'Dear little Ben, nothing would have made me happier than to see you again. In your heart, you know that's true. Every day that you dreamt of me is a day that I would have been dreaming of you.' She admires the view, sighs happily. 'It's so nice to be together again, isn't it? Just like before.' Ben wants to keep looking at her, to pretend that this moment is real, but his eyes are filling with tears. 'Benjamin, what's wrong?'

'Nothing,' he says, getting up and pacing off. 'I'm fine.' He stops some distance away, his mind full of all those years he spent as a young child: not knowing anything about his mother, not even knowing what she looked like; and all the while, the loneliness of living with two old people as his own behaviour became more and more erratic, until eventually he was put on medication, each pill serving as a daily reminder that he was

293

damaged goods. 'Do you know why I was in Grosvenor Square that day I met Alice? I'd been visiting the Memorial Garden, for September 11th. There's a little pavilion in there, with an inscription across the top that says "Grief is the price we pay for love". I go there sometimes to think of you. But whenever I read it, it just seems to me that I've only ever known the grief, not the love; I was left with all the pain of losing you, but none of the joy that's supposed to come before that.' He paces back towards her, barely even aware of the tears welling up from a sadness deep inside. 'The thing is, I've wanted this for so long, that's the problem. There isn't a single moment in my entire life that I haven't wanted to be with you again. I've thought of you every day for almost twenty years. Dreaming of what it would be like to see you and talk to you, to get a hug from you.' He gasps, the tears running down his face. 'And the worst thing is, for most of that time, I thought that if you really did come back, you'd only be disappointed in me. Ashamed of what I'd become, and what I hadn't become.'

'Oh, Benjamin…' He sees on her face the same pain he feels in his heart. 'Remember what I used to tell you every day: my love for you is like the sun. It's always shining, nothing can ever change that. Even when the days are gloomy, even in the middle of the night, the sun is always out there, shining just for you.'

The words bring back such a clear memory, it's as if he's a child again, back there in India with her, playing in the sunshine. 'I do remember that!' he says, smiling through his tears. 'I really do.' He wipes his face on his sleeve. 'I remember you saying it when we were—' but she's already gone.

Knightsbridge, London SW1

Despite having worked on parties like this before, it's the first time that Alice has also been allowed to attend. Standing there on the sidelines, she can't shake the feeling that she's in the engine room of a large ship, the machinery of spin in full motion all around her. Until a few hours ago, she'd thought nothing of the client's products, but now, as she looks out across the spectacle – the white-tied waiters, the sparkling lights, and Suzie Franklin, seeming to illuminate the event with her charisma – even Alice thinks she may buy some when she's next at the supermarket.

Geneva and Piers mingle as a couple, appearing so comfortable in one another's company, it's easy to imagine that they're best friends. For the umpteenth time, Alice watches as a photographer captures a picture of them with another of the many glamorous guests; both Geneva and Piers always holding garish canapés that they never eat. In the seconds that follow, Geneva beckons Alice over, surreptitiously passing their food to her yet again.

'Bring us some of the pink ones next,' she says. 'But take a bigger bite out of mine first.'

Alice hurriedly does as commanded, then retreats to the shadows, feeling obliged to finish Geneva's and Piers's food too; certain that creeping away to scrape them into a bin would send the wrong message.

'How many of those have you had already?' says Lucy, her headset making it look like she may burst into song at any moment.

'Too many,' replies Alice, through a full mouth. 'Have you noticed how Piers has spent half the evening running his hands through his hair, and the other half fiddling with his food? I've probably eaten a pound of hair wax by now.'

'I think grooming products are the least of your worries. Geneva says he's susceptible to lice.'

'Surely not?' replies Alice, her mouth still full. In the middle of the room, Piers once again runs a hand through his luxuriant head of hair. 'It looks very well kept, don't you think?'

'Apparently, that's exactly what they like. A beautiful home. Expensive products. It turns out that head lice are no different than the rest of us.'

Mid-chew, Alice spits everything into a napkin. 'You know what? I think I'm full.'

'Oh, poor Alice,' says Lucy, with a tone of genuine compassion. 'If only you'd learnt to say that years ago.'

★

'How are you holding up?' says Geneva, joining Alice on the sidelines later that evening.

'I feel a bit ill, to be honest.'

'Of course you do. It's your own fault for swallowing that filth.'

'I don't think we're supposed to say that about our client's products.'

'Nonsense, the client has bought my professional opinions, not my personal ones. I have no doubt that if I took even the smallest bite, I would blow it from both ends.'

They watch as, on the other side of the room, Suzie dances for the cameras, a bottle of sauce in each hand.

'I'm still amazed that you could get her,' says Alice. 'I can't imagine how you did it.'

'I know we've established that you can always find something positive to say, but I wonder if you're ready for the blood and guts of this business. For all those times when we get our hands really, really dirty.' She laughs. 'See, even the mention of it makes you look like a rabbit in headlights.'

'But I'm eager to learn. And isn't that why you hired me? To teach me how it all works.'

'All right then, here's a little test. What would you do if you happened to know some very unsavoury things about Suzie?'

'My God, you're *blackmailing* her?'

'I find your choice of words very disappointing. I'm *protecting* her, from herself.' She watches Suzie for a few moments, then turns back to Alice, evidently sees that she's still in shock. 'You're such an innocent…' She grabs a drink from a passing waiter, hands it to her.

'No, I shouldn't be drinking on the job.'

'For Christ's sake, Alice, at least pretend to be human.' Geneva stares at her until she starts to drink. 'There are always two sides to everything. In this instance, there's Suzie Franklin the national treasure, loved by families the length and breadth of Britain…' She catches Suzie's eye, gives her a smiling wave. 'And then there's Suzie Franklin the shameless slut, who I choose to keep on a very, very tight leash.'

'Does Piers know this?'

'Whose idea do you think it was?' She's distracted by a burst of light on the other side of the room, Suzie now transfigured by a sea of flashing cameras. 'This business is a hall of mirrors, Alice. You can either be the person crafting the lies, or the person believing them. I know who I'd rather be.'

*

Alice may have taken Geneva's advice a little too literally. In the last hour and a half, she's seized every opportunity to have another drink, watching through a growing veil of inebriation as the party started to fizzle out. Suzie has long since left the building, all the fun and glamour draining away with her, so that the room now feels more like a slaughterhouse at the end of a busy day, nothing to be done but hose down all the blood.

She's thinking of crawling under one of the tables to take a nap, but her head is so drenched in wine, she can't be certain that she hasn't done that already. She's still trying to piece together her memories of the evening when she realizes that Geneva and Piers are standing right in front of her, Piers giving her the same insincere but utterly convincing smile that he's been giving everyone all night. 'I bet you can't wait to get home to Ben and tell him all about the evening.'

'Oh, yes,' says Geneva. 'How is Ben?'

Alice resists the urge to steady herself against something. 'I feel the need to speak my mind,' she says, still clutching a glass of wine.

'That'll be a first,' replies Geneva.

'Trust me, you wouldn't say that if you knew what kind of week I've had.' Swaying slightly, she turns to Piers, trying not to slur her words. 'I know you're my boss. Hell, you're even my boss's boss. But all I want to say is this: you are a deceitful, manipulative letch.'

'Hear, hear,' says Geneva.

'And don't even get me started on *you*,' says Alice, turning to face her. 'I mean, forgive my French, but...' She takes another mouthful of wine. 'You are an evil cunt. *That's* how bad you are: even the c-word requires an adjective.'

After a long silence, Geneva turns to Piers. 'I never thought I'd say this, but we might make something of her yet.' Her poise as unruffled as ever, she starts to walk away, calling over her shoulder as she goes. 'See you on Monday, Alice.'

The Peak District

134 miles from Alice

Jeff and Karen appear to take it in their stride when Ben brings the urn down to breakfast with him, sitting it on the table amid the trappings of a leisurely Saturday morning.

'Shall I do you some fresh toast?' says Karen, as Ben takes a seat.

'No, I'm fine.'

'Please, allow me to fuss,' she says, already getting up. 'It makes me happy.'

Jeff speaks over the top of his newspaper. 'How are you feeling today?'

'I, er, followed your advice and had a chat, with *you know who*. She helped me remember something important. Something really important.'

Jeff gives him a wink and goes back to his paper.

'And what are your plans for the day?' says Karen, putting a fresh pot of tea on the table.

'I'm going to head out with my granddad again.'

'There are some lovely hikes nearby,' she replies. 'Win Hill is very pretty.'

'Win Hill. I love the name.'

'It's just on the other side of Hope, would you believe it? The village of Hope, that is. You basically just head to Hope and keep climbing. It's good advice for life, when you think about it.'

'It sounds nice, but I've already decided to go back to the hill I climbed yesterday.'

'Oh, yes? Which one was that?'

'I don't know, it was somewhere over there,' says Ben, pointing in the vague direction of the kitchen sink. 'I've decided to scatter my grandfather's ashes up there.' Karen stops what she's doing, and even Jeff lowers his newspaper. 'As soon as I woke up this morning, I knew it was the right thing to do. I know it's what he would have wanted.'

He notices Karen glance at Jeff, imagines that she's concerned, but then she's speaking, her voice gentle and reassuring. 'I think that's a lovely thing to do. Everyone deserves to be laid to rest somewhere beautiful.'

'And it is beautiful up there,' says Ben. 'Special too. It's… well, it's complicated, but it will always be a special place to me.'

'You should eat up if you're planning a big day,' she says, fetching him a mountainous plate of food. 'You'll need your energy out there.'

'I doubt I'll need *this* much energy, but thank you.'

He's busy eating when he realizes that Jeff and Karen are watching him, this childless couple seeming to find pleasure in his mere presence. Karen immediately pretends to be doing something else, while Jeff lurches into conversation.

'I'll, er, dig out some maps for you, if you want, just so you know all the other places round here. There's lots to see. Enough for a lifetime, I'd say.'

Feltham, West London

Rachel calls while Alice is still lying in bed, doubtless wanting to hear that Alice mentioned her to Suzie Franklin last night; that Suzie now wants to hear Rachel's demo tape; that she plans to make her a star.

'The whole evening was totally surreal,' says Alice. 'I've always really liked Suzie, but now she just seems like some bullied circus animal, endlessly jumping through hoops because she can't say no.'

'At least she's famous.'

'Do you genuinely not care? Are you not in the least bit bothered by the morality of it all?'

'I wouldn't mind if someone bullied me into being a celebrity.'

'Look,' says Alice, closing her eyes and willing Rachel to disappear, 'it was a long night. I don't think I have the energy for this conversation.'

'Let's meet for lunch instead.'

'You know what? I'd rather not.'

'Don't tell me you're meeting the vegan. He's *never* going to talk to you again.'

'Thank you, Rachel. And no, I'm not meeting the vegan.'

'Oh my God, it's Ben again, isn't it? He's totally wrong for you.'

'Excuse me?'

'I've never told you this, but I have very strong instincts about Ben. It's like a psychic thing.'

'Rachel—'

'The truth is, you've changed since Ben came into your life. I didn't want to say anything before, but it's been very obvious to me for the last few weeks that he's coming between us.'

'All this because I won't meet you for lunch?'

'Like I said, Alice, it's a psychic thing. It's not *me* saying that Ben is wrong for you, it's the universe. I'm just a messenger of the truth. It's like I've been ordained to do this, as a sort of intervention.'

'You can't sing,' snaps Alice. There's a tense silence at the other end of the line. 'There, I've said it. I've wanted to say it

303

for ages. I can't stand your bloody voice. It's like listening to a small furry animal die.'

'See, this is my point. Ben's changed you. I don't even know who you are anymore. It's him or me, Alice. You have to choose.'

'What, like this?' she says, hanging up.

The Peak District
136 miles from Alice

The farm is long since out of sight when Ben stops to call Dave. It takes him a while to find a decent signal, pausing here and there beside fields of grazing sheep. As he waits for the call to connect, he leans against an old stone wall; empty fields spread out before him, grey clouds gathering overhead.

When Dave finally answers, his voice is thick with sleep. 'Ben, mate. Is everything all right?'

'I'm out for the day with Granddad.'

'Okay, that's nice.'

'And I've decided to stop the ride.'

Dave instantly sounds more awake. 'Has anything happened?'

'Nothing's wrong,' he replies. 'It's just I understand now why I started this ride. Why I wanted to find Alice in the first place. I was a bit lost, wasn't I? It's like I went looking for something without knowing what it was.'

'Ben, this is all quite deep for first thing on a Saturday morning.'

'What I'm trying to say is, I don't feel lost anymore. I've decided to stay up here a while. I've already got a job, and a place to live.'

'Christ, that was quick.'

'But it feels right. Though I do feel a bit bad about Agnes's bike. She won't get it back for ages.'

'Mate, she's already started growing. Give it another month or two and she won't fit through the door, let alone on a bike.' Ben can hear Agnes too now, mumbling something. 'She says we might be able to feel the baby kick next month.'

Ben smiles at the thought of them: a ready-made family sprawled on the bed sheets, simply waiting for the months to work their magic. 'It's funny, ever since you told me about you and Agnes, I thought I was losing you somehow. And now I can see I'm not losing anything, am I? I'm just getting even more.'

'That's right, mate, you are. And you're going to be a great godfather.'

'I hate to admit it, but on this occasion you're right.' He thinks of the many ways in which the coming years will be full of love and joy. 'I think you'll find that I'm going to be the greatest godfather the world has ever known.'

The 11:06 to London Waterloo

There's something therapeutic about making this journey on a weekend. From Monday to Friday, this train is a crowded reminder that nothing about adult life is as easy or as pleasurable as Alice had once hoped, but today she has no problem getting a seat, gazing across the rooftops of London as the train hurries eastwards. Even Waterloo has a relaxed air this morning, everyone seeming to take more time over life's pleasurable details: the aroma of fresh coffee; the scent of croissants hot from the oven. By the time she reaches Grosvenor Square, it's hard to remember why she complains so often about this journey, this city. It's as though her everyday life has been turned inside out, and at last she can see its true beauty.

She enters the garden and goes straight to the bench where she met Ben all those weeks ago. Taking a seat, she quietly wishes him well wherever he may be; gives thanks for the way he walked into her life, with nothing but some kind words and a gentle smile.

When her phone starts to ring, she doesn't even look at it at first, certain that it can only be Rachel, even more neurotic now that she's had time to ponder what she's done. But then she glances down and sees that it's not Rachel's name on the screen, it's Chris's.

'Oh, God,' she says, the ringing growing louder while she wavers, desperate to answer the call, but terrified of the conversation that may follow. In those final seconds she again thinks of Ben; how he'd tell her to take the call because she's beautiful and deserving of happiness.

And so she does.

Stanage Edge, The Peak District
141 miles from Alice

Although it's a Saturday, grey skies and the threat of rain have kept everyone indoors this morning. As Ben climbs the hill, following the same path as yesterday, he thinks of all the years his grandfather spent in Korea; how he must have struggled through the summer months, quietly longing for the cool, damp air of England.

'There's plenty of that today,' he says, quickening his pace as the land rises upwards.

Climbing into the cloud, it's easy to imagine that he's not taking his grandfather's ashes to a mere mountaintop, but is rather ascending to heaven itself to deliver his grandfather into the care of the gods.

'I entrust him to you,' Ben will tell them, as he hands over the ashes. 'This is a good man who lived a good life.'

As he nears the top of the hill, the clouds begin to break,

and snatches of blue sky come into view, shafts of sunlight illuminating the landscape below.

Standing on the same rock where he ate lunch yesterday, he takes the urn from his backpack, unscrewing the lid in a reverent silence. At first he thinks he should say something profound, but then he remembers how his grandfather lived his life: a man of actions rather than words; a man whose feelings were no less strong for being unspoken.

Ben gently tips the urn, worrying for an instant that the ashes will simply fall at his feet, but then the wind is catching them and carrying them aloft. 'So long, Granddad. Rest in peace.'

He's watching as the grey cloud drifts out across the landscape, fading with every passing second, when Alice appears by his side in a flurry of yellow. 'I should go too,' she says. 'Your granddad could probably do with someone to show him around. And I dare say he'd like a lemon bonbon, wouldn't he? Everyone loves a lemon bonbon.' Her face lights up in a smile that Ben remembers well now; a smile that he will never forget. 'Goodbye, my sweet little Benjamin.'

He calls to her as she begins to float out across the landscape. 'Will I ever see you again?'

She shakes her head, but still that same beautiful smile. 'Your life is full of sunshine, Ben. It will always be full of sunshine.'

Day

1

One month earlier

Grosvenor Square Garden, London W1

Face to face with Ben

Everyone else in the park seems to be relishing the day, basking in a rare moment of warmth, but not Alice. She sits alone on a bench, her only solace a large portion of French fries. Having already been told by Geneva this morning that she's looking fat, she's forsaken the ketchup, would forsake the fries too if only they weren't the first good thing about the day, every taste like a warm hug.

She's just attempted a particularly ambitious mouthful when she realizes that a young man has stopped right in front of her, a radiant smile on his face. 'You're like something from a mail-order catalogue,' he says, 'but even more beautiful than that. Just looking at you makes me feel all warm and fuzzy inside. And I mean that in a good way, not like a hot flush or something. Not that I've ever had one. Though I think my gran has.' Still chewing through her mouthful of fries, Alice says nothing. Perhaps mistaking her silence for concern, he speaks again. 'Whatever I just said, ignore it. Unless it was, you know, *normal*, in which case don't.' He takes a deep breath, appears to compose himself. 'What I'm trying to say is, I'm Ben. And I think you're beautiful. Very, very beautiful.'

'Thank you,' she says, finally free to speak. 'That's very sweet of you.'

'And don't worry, you don't have to tell me your name,

not if you don't want to. You can never be too careful with strangers, can you?' An elderly man passes them, walking a dachshund on a leash. 'That's the problem with London. One minute you could be talking to some sweet old man like that, and the next he's flashing his bits at you.' The man looks askance. 'Not that this bloke ever has, I hasten to add, but even in a neighbourhood like this, you have to be careful. Especially someone as beautiful as you.' He looks down at his feet, seems bashful now. 'I didn't mean to disturb your lunch. I should probably get going…'

'I'm Alice,' she says, as he turns to leave. 'And thank you for the compliment. You've made my day.'

His face lights up, with a childlike wonder. 'Well, you can keep it with you now, can't you? Anytime you're feeling a bit low, you can just remember that Ben says you're beautiful.'

Geneva appears from nowhere, Harry tucked under her arm. 'Alice, what's going on here?'

'Everything's fine,' she replies.

Ben turns to Geneva, seemingly as horrified by her as she is by him. 'You're a bit scary, aren't you?' And now an apologetic shrug. 'Me and my motor mouth! Imagine how bad I'd be if I *wasn't* on medication.'

Looking aghast, Geneva herds Alice from the bench. 'Come along, we should be getting you back to Glasgow.'

'You live in Glasgow?' says Ben.

Alice hesitates, unsure how to explain it.

'Yes, she does,' says Geneva, clearly taking too much pleasure in the words. 'And it's time she got back there.'

'Thank you for all the kind things you said,' Alice tells him, as Geneva urges her away. 'It was very nice to meet you.'

They're some distance across the square when Alice glances back and sees that Ben is still standing there; still gazing at her with such an expression that, for the very first time in her life, it really does seem possible that she's perfect just the way she is.

Acknowledgements

Behind every published author is a team of talented and hard-working people. I offer my heartfelt thanks to everyone at Little, Brown, especially James Gurbutt and Sarah Castleton for their kindness, humour and wisdom.

I would also like to offer my thanks to the many wonderful people I have the privilege of calling friends: Dirk Feldhaus and Jan von Holleben, Robert Kugler, Harald Niederstraßer, Tim Bertko, Rico Wagner, Christoph Abeling, Cassie Lefebvre, Stefano Santangelo, Fabio Cozzalupi, Heinz-Dieter Kämmerer, Marco Rosenwasser, Ewa Deja, Lars and Betti Schlorf, Juka Enns, Michi and Hiro Matsuzaki, Daniel Lavoie and Xavier Gurza, Javier Garcia Agut, David Lopez Perez, Motty Vaknin, Jose Cabanas, Jucélio Matos, Soon-En Wong and Bruce Foreman, and Reinhold Kreifelts and David Lam. Thanks likewise to my Little Italy in Berlin - Marghe, Enrico and Flora − for constant laughter and the best possible kind of madness, and to M. Schäfer for being the perfect neighbour.

I will always be grateful that my long and circuitous journey to representation, from Shanghai to New York to London, finally brought me to the desk of Juliet Mushens. Her passion for storytelling, her natural talent for the job and her flair for leopard print are a constant inspiration to everyone who knows her.

The writing of this book coincided with a personal crisis that led to a significant delay in its completion. I'm deeply thankful to my publisher for giving me the space and time that I needed to deal with my depression. Most of all I was lucky to find the right therapeutic support on my long journey of self-acceptance, faint echoes of which began to redefine the telling of Ben and Alice's story. Looking back, it's no coincidence that all the early drafts of this book had a dark and tragic ending. I think it was only when I was able to believe in a happy ending for myself that I was able to create one for Ben and Alice too. I will always be grateful to the extraordinary talents of Dr Christian Dombrowe, who so skilfully helped me re-read and make sense of my own life story. Without him, neither this book nor I would be here.